HARBOUR THIEVES

BILL FREEMAN

James Lorimer & Company, Publishers
Toronto 1984

ISBN 0-88862-746-7 paper
    0-88862-747-5 cloth

Cover design: Don Fernley
Cover painting: Cecily Moon
Map: Dave Hunter
All illustrations are reproduced courtesy Metropolitan Toronto Library Board, except: *Picton* and *Chicora* at dock (Archives of Ontario); police constable and detective (Metropolitan Toronto Police Museum) and sailboats at Toronto Islands (Royal Ontario Museum).

Canadian Cataloguing in Publication Data
Freeman, Bill, 1938-
  Harbour thieves
(Adventures in Canadian history)
I. Title. II. Series: Freeman, Bill, 1938-
Adventures in Canadian history.

PS8561.R378H37 1984   jC813'.54   C84-099473-7
PZ7.F73Ha 1984

James Lorimer & Company, Publishers
Egerton Ryerson Memorial Building
35 Britain Street
Toronto, Ontario M5A IR7

Printed and bound in Canada

Toronto in the 1870s was a city where some people had enough wealth to live in luxury while the great majority suffered terrible poverty. The poorest of all were the street urchins — the dozens of children who struggled to support themselves by selling newspapers, shining shoes, running errands, and, occasionally, stealing. With starvation dogging their heels, and the police watching their every move in the belief they were all criminals, it was not an easy life.

The lives of Toronto's street children in the last century provide the background for *Harbour Thieves*. It is a work of fiction, but the children's struggles in the city's streets, prisons and police courts are part of the real history of Canada.

Bill Freeman

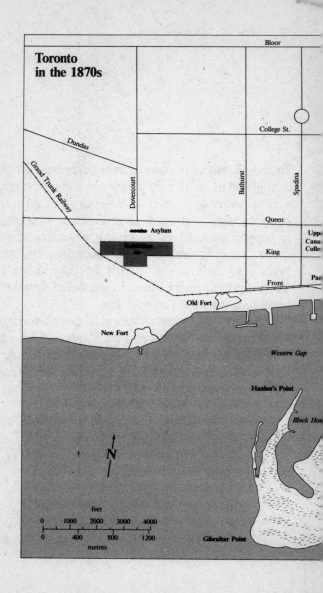

Toronto in the 1870s

Bloor

College St.

Dundas

Grand Trunk Railway

Dovercourt

Bathurst

Spadina

Queen

Asylum

Exhibition

Upp
Cana
Colle

King

Front

Pa

Old Fort

New Fort

Western Gap

Hanlan's Point

Block Hou

N

feet

| 0 | 1000 | 2000 | 3000 | 4000 |

| 0 | 400 | 800 | 1200 |

metres

Gibraltar Point

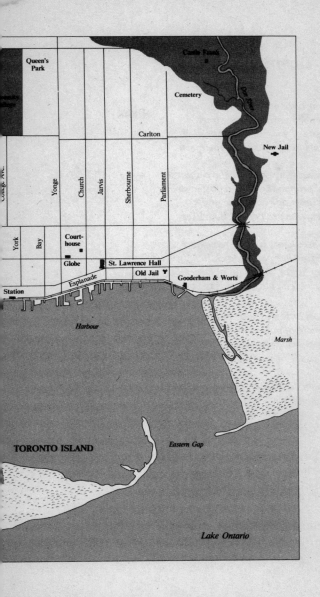

Queen's Park

Castle Frank

Cemetery

Don River

Carlton

New Jail

College Ave.

Yonge

Church

Jarvis

Sherbourne

Parliament

York

Bay

Courthouse

Globe

St. Lawrence Hall

Old Jail

Gooderham & Worts

Esplanade

Station

Harbour

Marsh

TORONTO ISLAND

Eastern Gap

Lake Ontario

The Toronto Newsboy

The poor little newsboy that jostles
The parsons parading the street,
Is not one of your sucking Apostles,
No Saints in his class will you meet.

He is honest; his wits are the brightest,
And his prompt thrust of repartee strikes;
But his language is not the politest;
He can swear pretty hard if he likes.

Yet a warm heart is his. I remember
Now selling her papers, a child
On King Street, one night in December,
When the bleak blast from Bay Street blew wild.

Some lost little waif she resembled,
Her bundle of papers unsold;
Till one newsboy, who saw how she trembled,
"See, boys!" he said, "Sissie is cold!"

They clubbed all their coppers together,
They bought every paper she had,
And they wrapped her up warm from the weather,
And sent her home hearty and glad.

Though scarcely thought worthy to jostle
Your parsons parading the street;
Though by no means a sucking Apostle
A Man in each newsboy you'll meet!

C. Pelhamp Mulvany,
Toronto Past and Present Until 1882

CHAPTER 1

THE passenger car swayed and the steel wheels clacked on the rails as the Grand Trunk train from Montreal made its way slowly along the track. Smoke from the big engine belched black and sooty, sometimes almost obscuring the view of the southern Ontario fields being prepared for planting. People in the third-class coach car sat on hard wooden benches, listening to Murphy, the big Irishman, talk in his loud musical accent.

"Bejesus if Toronto isn't a tedious place of temperance, tidiness and Toryism. A place of sober Sundays where the Orange Lodge sets all the rules. A dreadful place. Still, it's a wealthy city where a poor man like meself can scheme and dream of finding riches."

Jamie and Meg Bains knew the Irishman only too well. That winter they had worked for him at Lachine Mill in Montreal and had suffered from his glib tongue and explosive temper. To Jamie, having Murphy on the train was a bad sign.

Things would still be a struggle in Toronto. They would have to find work as soon as they got to the city so they could send money back to their mother in Ottawa to help support the family. In that year of 1875 hard times had settled on the country. There were a lot of unemployed people looking for work. It would not be easy. And now, to have Murphy …

The Irishman, sitting in the seat ahead of them, was talking again in a loud voice, but Jamie wasn't listening. The boy stared at the outline of Murphy's broad shoulders and studied the ruddy face partly covered by long muttonchop whiskers and a drooping moustache.

"Do you think Murphy is following us to Toronto, Meg?" he whispered to his sister.

"No, it's just a coincidence that we're on the same train."

Jamie looked worried. He was dressed in workman's clothes of dark jacket, long pants and heavy work boots. The shaggy brown hair sticking out from under his cap, his smooth skin and open blue eyes made him look younger than twelve. "He must hate us after what happened at the Mill."

"But he wouldn't follow us all the way to Toronto because of that." Meg was more certain. She was only fourteen, but her years of hard work in lumber camps, aboard ships and in factories had given her strong, square shoulders and a straightforward confidence. A pretty girl with dark eyes and light hair tied neatly in a bun, she wore a simple blouse, shawl and cotton skirt down to her ankles.

"We'll be in Toronto soon," announced a blue-coated conductor who had come into the car. "Would you return to your own seats now, please?"

Murphy got to his feet and stretched. A freshly lit cigar glowed in the side of his mouth. "Got to get back to first class where I belong," he said to no one in particular. Then he stared straight at Jamie and Meg, stepped forward and bent down quickly. "Once again I cross paths with my two lovelies." The smell of strong drink and cigar smoke was overpowering. "Looks like things are not settled between us yet." And then he was gone.

As Jamie stared after the disappearing hulk, he felt panic grow in the pit of his stomach, but then he heard one of the other passengers. "Look! There she is. The Don River and marsh."

The train crossed a brown sluggish river on a wooden bridge and then curved towards the waterfront. To the south they could see a large marsh with swaying bulrushes and conical-shaped muskrat houses. From the other window they had their first glimpse of the city. Terraced houses lined the streets. Then they passed a huge red-bricked structure with a tall chimney sending up a column of smoke which someone said was the Toronto Rolling Mills. As they banked around a gentle curve suddenly they got a full view of the harbour.

It was a warm day in late spring with a bright sun gleaming off the still waters of the harbour. Out about a half a mile they could see a chain of low islands. There were sailboats running before a gentle breeze, cargo schooners rode at anchor and a boy was rowing a skiff as he trawled with a fishing rod propped in the stern.

"Look! Isn't she a beauty?" Jamie said, pointing at a big side-wheeled riverboat painted a gleaming white with smart black trim. A tall smokestack stood amidships and rows of windows marked the passengers' cabins and the luxurious dining salons. "If I was rich that's the way I would have wanted to come to Toronto."

The train glided past a grey-stoned building marked Gooderham and Worts Distillery, and then suddenly a big sombre-looking prison with bars on its half-moon-shaped windows loomed on the right like a threatening fortress. Then it was gone. They were in the midst of a whole collection of wharfs and warehouses that crowded the water's edge. The jetties were jammed with boats of every description. There was a schooner off-loading a cargo of barrels with a horse and pulley system attached to the rigging. A number of steamboats were tied up taking on passengers and cargo. Meg even spotted a sleek, white screw-driven vessel, a rare sight on the lakes. Coal from an old scow was being unloaded into a boxcar, and a small ship with square sails on her forward mast was riding at anchor.

The train slowed as it was shunted through a series of switches. Somewhere a bell was ringing and one of the railway men called out instructions. People in the third-class coach began collecting their bags and stood in the aisles waiting to get off the train. Meg wrestled their carpet bag and canvas sack out of the overhead rack and then she and Jamie peered through the window towards the city.

The land rose gently from the harbour front. Buildings were tightly cramped together with streets slashing through them every two hundred paces or more. Most were square brick structures, but the skyline was broken with the domes of the public buildings and the spires of churches.

Now they could see the two massive towers of the new station, and slowly the train eased its way into the building. "Union Station. Toronto's Union Station," called out the conductor from the back of the coach car. The train eased to a stop.

The packed crowd pressed forward. "Mind your step, now." The conductor reached up to help Meg down from the high step, and Jamie scrambled after.

It was a relief to get outside once again after twelve hours cooped up in the coach car. The boy looked around. The station was a magnificent building, big enough to bring the entire train under its roof. There were long walls with elegant windows and overhead the roof was supported by a complex network of steel girders and a huge skylight running the entire length of the building.

"Come on, Jamie," Meg snapped. "We've got a lot to do if we're to get settled before dark."

The boy hoisted his canvas bag over his shoulder and hurried to keep up with his sister. There was just too much to see. They passed the steam engine wheezing and snorting — still belching strong smoke from its bulbous stack. Jamie was fascinated by the giant wheels and complicated mechanisms fixed underneath the big black boiler. Out in front was a huge cow-catcher and above that sat the brass lantern polished and gleaming.

"Come on. Keep up," urged Meg, and the boy ran after her.

Throngs of people from the Montreal train streamed through the gate and into the main waiting room. Now the place was a mass of humanity with people greeting friends and relatives. Newsboys shouted out headlines. Porters with carts stacked high with baggage steered their way through the throng. There were beggars holding their caps out and girls selling flowers from wicker baskets. Railwaymen dressed in heavy overalls stood beside ladies and gentlemen in the most fashionable attire. It was a scene of mass confusion, and Jamie couldn't get enough of it.

Suddenly there was a loud familiar voice behind them. It was Murphy, his bowler hat set firmly on his head, walking stick in hand. "And may this town give you street rats what you deserve." As he strode away after his porter carrying his belongings, they could hear his laughter.

"What's he mean by that?" Jamie asked nervously.

"Who knows what Murphy means?" Meg looked annoyed. "Come on. We have to move if we're going to find a place to live."

The girl hoisted up the big carpet bag and began striding briskly across the waiting room, clomping along in her boots. She pushed open a door with her shoulder and the two of them were out on the street.

Hansom cabs lined the curb, the big black horses calmly waiting as their masters bartered a fare. A driver shouted to Meg, but the girl only shook her head and hurried on. Out near the main entrance to the station, large stages from the hotels with red plush seats were loading passengers. Wagons and groups of people crowded roads and sidewalks.

Suddenly Meg stopped, set her bag on the ground and struggled to get a piece of paper out of her skirt pocket. Jamie looked over her shoulder at the scribbled note.

"Elliot's Row. That's what the lady on the train said was the cheapest lodgings in Toronto. South side of King Street between York and Simcoe." She studied the nearest street sign for a moment and announced, "York Street is right here, and the lake is behind us. All we have to do is follow this street north."

She was folding the piece of paper when suddenly a young slip of a boy no more than ten with a ragged shirt, short pants, worn-out shoes and dirty face swept down on them as quickly and quietly as a cat. In an instant he had grabbed the carpet bag Meg had left on the ground and dashed off with it.

"What are you doing?" the girl shouted. "Come back with that!" She ran after the thief as fast as she could.

When Jamie understood what had happened he sprinted after them. The bag he was carrying bounced awkwardly against his shoulder.

The thief had a good five paces on them, and he was fast, but when he glanced back and saw two people pursuing him, the wild look in his eyes turned to fear and then terror.

Meg and Jamie were determined. Most of what they owned in the world was in that bag, and they had to get it back. Meg ran as fast as she could in her long skirt. Jamie was right behind, gaining with every pace. Then the two of them were running together — running the frightened thief into the ground.

The heavy bag was bumping awkwardly against the young boy's legs. He did not have the strength to carry the bag and outrun them. Now the gap was closing. In desperation the boy dashed out onto the road. A horse pulling a wagon shied in fright. The boy veered to save himself and Jamie and Meg grabbed him at the same time.

"What are you doing?" Meg shouted angrily.

"Don't hit me! Please don't hit me!" cowered the boy. He was small and very frightened.

Jamie wrenched the carpet bag out of his hand. "Why are you stealing?"

"Don't hurt me, please. I didn't mean to do it."

"What sort of an excuse is that? You stole our bag!"

"Please, please. I didn't mean to do it. Don't report me to the police. I'll go to jail for sure." Tears were forming in his eyes.

Suddenly a big voice boomed. "What's going on here?" The three young people looked up to find a large policeman with a curled moustache, high helmet and long blue coat with brass buttons down the front. "Why were you chasing this boy?"

Jamie glanced at his sister for just a moment and then looked again at the small person in the tattered outfit. The boy's eyes were wide, his lips trembling. He looked desperately about.

"Ah ... ah ... it's nothing, sir," said Jamie trying hard to be natural.

"Nothing? You were chasing this boy. He stole your bag. I saw it."

Again Jamie glanced at his sister. "It was just a game, sir." He smiled weakly. "We were playing a game. He took our bag, and we chased after him."

The policeman's eyes widened in disbelief and then his face turned stern.

"He's right," Meg added. "It was just a game, officer. We're sorry if we caused any problems."

The policeman twisted his moustache for a moment. "All right," he said slowly. "If that's your story then get going but let me warn all three of you that the police department is watching. The least problem — the least bit of trouble — and you'll be cooling your heels in that big stone jail we've got in the east end of town. Now be off with you." The big blue-coated man turned and walked back towards the train station swinging his night stick in his hand.

"Come on. Let's get out of here quick," Meg whispered to her brother. The two of them picked up their bags and started heading up York Street.

They had gone no more than a few paces when they heard a voice behind them. "Ah … I don't know how to thank you." The boy was following them up the street. "The police, they … they watch us all the time and … they've said that if they take us to court again the judge is going to send us to jail for years. You saved me."

Then he stopped as if he had run out of things to say. Another boy dressed in the same type of ragged clothes had been trailing behind. He came up and the two stood side by side looking at Meg and Jamie out of sad eyes. The boy who had stolen from them was the taller and more talkative of the two. His friend was very young looking, no more than eight. Jamie and Meg stopped and the four stared at each other for a long moment.

Meg smiled. "Maybe you can help us. We're trying to find a place called Elliot's Row. It's supposed to be up on King and York streets somewhere. Do you know it?"

"Sure we do," said the smaller boy. "I used to live there. It's a terrible place."

"We need cheap lodgings. We just came in from Montreal and we don't have much money. Can you take us?"

The boy flashed a grin. "Sure. It's not far up York Street here."

The two street boys led the way. After a few moments one of them looked back. "Want help carrying your bag?"

Jamie laughed. "Don't think so. You're a little too fast of foot for us." And they all giggled.

They went up York and crossed Front Street, dodging wagons, men on horseback and carriages. The Queen's Hotel, a magnificent four-storey building with an impressive pillared entrance was just down the street, and they passed the Rossin House, a large square-shaped hotel. Shops lined the streets and the taverns were doing a brisk business.

The two boys chatted in an open, friendly way. "I'm Paddy," explained the taller boy. "This is my friend, Bud. We sell newspapers, shine shoes and do odd jobs about town."

"Don't you go to school?" asked Meg.

"No, school's just a waste of time."

"Do you know of any jobs we can do in Toronto?"

"There's lots of unemployment. Some people are starving," replied Bud. "But us kids can always sell newspapers."

Meg thought for a moment. "We could do that until we get something better. What do you think, Jamie?"

"All right by me."

"We could help you get set up. Tell you the best corners and things like that," said Paddy.

"Would you?"

"Sure. You saved me from the coppers."

So it was agreed that the next morning at six the four of them would meet at the *Globe* newspaper office. The two street boys showed them where to find the landlord who looked after Elliot's Row and then disappeared.

The place was a dilapidated tenement built flush up against the sidewalk. Playing outside on the street were a dozen children, most in bare feet and scruffy clothing. Windows were broken, hallways were thick with accumulated dirt and the building looked as if it had never had a coat of paint.

But despite the appearance of the place, minutes after they arrived Jamie and Meg found themselves in possession of a single room with two narrow cots, a wash basin, small table with a stump of a candle and two hard-backed chairs. The walls were a grey grime, bare of any decoration. The door would only close by putting a shoulder to it, the windows were filthy and three of the four panes were cracked.

Jamie sat down on his cot and felt the sagging mattress. Slowly he surveyed the room and then smiled weakly at his sister. "At least there's one good thing. Mother has never known how terrible things have been for us."

CHAPTER 2

IT didn't take long for Meg and Jamie to get to the *Globe* office the next morning. All they had to do was walk due east along the King Street boardwalk, past the fancy restaurants and elegant shops displaying fine goods in their windows. They crossed Bay and Yonge streets, and there was the imposing building that housed the *Globe*.

The roar and clatter of the presses grew louder as they went around to the back of the building to find the door where the newsboys got their papers. In the yard, wagons were lined up in single file. Men came out of big double doors carrying stacks of newspapers hot off the presses and piled them into the back of the front wagon. Once it was loaded the driver touched his horse with the reins, it moved off at a good pace and the next wagon moved up.

Meg and Jamie saw two boys and a girl disappear through one of the back doors, and they knew that was the place they were looking for. Inside they found a room filled with twenty or thirty street kids, as scruffy a group as they had ever seen. Five or six were girls and the rest were young boys ranging in age between nine and about sixteen. Some had no shoes, many had shirts with big rips and almost all looked dirty. They were a rough-looking lot, filled with a swaggering confidence that bordered on outright defiance.

The news vendors were in only one part of the huge printing shop of the *Globe*. Behind a long counter they could see the presses — big, black complicated machines that rattled and thumped and shook the whole building. Along one wall were several typographical machines where the printers set the type, and in another section were long canvas-topped tables where the pages were laid out. Printers and pressmen were hurrying about tending the machines, as the foremen shouted and men ran frantically as they tried to haul away the stacks of papers that the presses kept spewing out.

The young people had formed a line waiting for their papers, and Jamie and Meg joined the end of it. Bud and Paddy were ahead of them, but the two boys left their places to come and explain how things worked. They almost had to shout to be heard over the noise of the presses.

"They load the wagons first," said Paddy. "It'll be a few minutes before we get our own papers. Better get your money out. You've got to pay two and three-quarters cents for every paper you get."

"Then how do you make money?" asked Jamie innocently.

"You sell the papers for three cents a copy and pocket the difference."

"It's not much. A quarter cent a paper. Could starve."

"A lot do."

Meg had her change purse out and was carefully extracting a few of their hard-earned coins. "How many papers do you think we can sell?" she asked.

"Depends on how hard you work. You've got to really run after the customer," answered Bud.

Paddy seemed better organized. "Why don't you get fifty each? You don't have a corner and you might find it hard to sell them."

"A corner?" asked Jamie. "What's that mean?"

"Most of us have one spot where we go every day so we get regular customers who buy from us, but you're going to have to move around until you find a good place."

As they were chatting, the door to the street opened and a tall, rangy boy of about sixteen came into the room. His hair was sun bleached and his complexion ruddy. The clothes he wore were as scruffy as any of the others, but he sported what looked like a new pair of suspenders. For a moment he stood by the door with his hands on his hips, watching the scene with dark, arrogant eyes. Then he swaggered to the end of the line where Jamie was standing.

"Hi, Stinger," said Bud. "How are you doin'?"

The new boy gave a curt nod and then studied the room in a detached way. The others went back to their conversation.

"You've got to really work hard the first couple of hours," Paddy was saying. "If you can't sell all of your papers then you'll get stuck with them and lose a lot of money. Everything has to be sold to make a profit."

Jamie had stepped out of line to listen to the conversation. When there was a lull he moved back into line just in front of Stinger.

"Where do you think you're goin', kid?" The big boy bristled.

Jamie smiled weakly. "This is my place in line."

"You lost your place. You stepped out of line and now you're behind me."

"No, I was just listening. This was my place."

"Sorry, buddy." There was a snarl in Stinger's words. "You left your place in line so now you go to the very end. That's the rules around here."

Other newsboys had overheard and they started to crowd around in expectation of a fight. Jamie felt trapped. Stinger loomed over him. The young boy didn't stand much of a chance, but he wouldn't back down. "I didn't leave the line. I didn't do anything."

"You lost your place, kid. Now get to the end."

"But I was just talking."

"Get to the back!"

"No! This is my place!"

A smile twisted on Stinger's face. "Think you're one of the big ones, do you?"

"Fight!" someone said. The other kids were drawn to the action like a magnet. "It's Stinger in a fight!"

Jamie had planted himself stubbornly in his place and refused to move.

"You're behind me, kid!" Suddenly Stinger grabbed Jamie by the front of the coat and tried to push him.

"Leave me alone." The boy struggled and twisted until he broke free.

"There's a fight." "Give it to him, Stinger!" Kids were screaming.

Meg forced herself between the two boys. "Leave my brother alone!"

Stinger tried to push past the girl and get at Jamie. "Get out of my way!"

"Stay out of this, Meg!" shouted Jamie.

"Let me get at the little runt!"

"Why don't you pick on someone your own size, Stinger?" came a deep male voice from outside the circle of onlookers. The action suddenly froze. It was a bowler-hatted man. He was tall and clean shaven in a neat, woollen, three-piece suit.

"Moffat! Detective Moffat!" someone said.

"Always causing problems, Stinger. Why is it that I always find you at the centre of trouble?"

"I don't cause no trouble." The boy had turned sullen and wary.

"Really? That's not what your police record says." The detective stood with his hands behind his back. Newsboys scuttled out of his way. "What about the break-in last night?" he demanded sharply.

"What break-in? You can't pin me with that."

"Where were you around ten o'clock?"

"I was home in bed."

"And where's home these days?" Moffat stopped in front of the boy and stared intently at him.

"I got lodgings over on Sherbourne Street. But I don't have to tell you coppers where I live."

"What are you trying to cover up, Stinger? What are you frightened of?"

"Nothin'. Why don't you flat-foots just leave me alone?"

The detective had his hands on his hips. "If you stay honest then you won't have anything to worry about." Slowly he turned on his heel.

The street vendors quietly resumed their line again. As the detective walked around he nodded to some and spoke to others. It seemed every one of them had come into contact with him at some time. When he saw Paddy he paused.

"Was it you that tried to steal the bag at the train station yesterday, Pat?"

The young boy was in a sudden panic. "No, I didn't steal nothin', sir. It was just a game."

"A game? The policeman's report that I saw said you stole the bag and then found some kids to help you lie your way out of it. What's the truth, Paddy?"

"But I'm telling the truth, sir. Ask Meg or Jamie here. They'll tell you."

The detective turned to them suspiciously. Slowly he began walking around them. "What do you know about it?"

"Paddy's right," said Jamie nervously. "He didn't steal the bag. We were just playing."

Moffat was quiet for a moment, studying the two of them carefully. "Jamie and Meg what?" he asked. "What's your last name?"

"Bains, sir," Meg replied.

"Where are you from?"

"We just came from Montreal, but originally we're from Ottawa."

"Drifters. Vagabonds. Just like all the others."

"We're looking for work," Meg added. "Selling papers is just temporary."

He nodded skeptically. "Just stay out of trouble. That's all we ask. Toronto has a reputation for not being very nice to those that break the law."

"Yes, sir," Jamie answered. "Don't worry about us, sir."

A moment later the detective was focusing again on the broad-shouldered boy waiting just behind Jamie. "So, can you prove you were at home last night, Stinger?"

"Why do you always pick on me? Get off my tail."

"Take it easy, Stinger." The detective smiled. "If I didn't know any better I'd think you were anxious to cover something up."

The newspapers were coming out now. Big stacks of them were slapped down on the counter and the line began moving forward. The boys and girls told the man how many papers they wanted, he rapidly counted them, money was exchanged and the news vendors hurried out, anxious to get on the street and start selling.

As the line moved forward Moffat was left behind watching the scene with his hands behind his back. Jamie overheard Stinger mutter, "That copper knows too much about what's going on."

Meg paid the man at the counter for a hundred papers. They were counted out in two stacks, then she and Jamie each grabbed a bunch and headed for the street.

It was a small paper of eight pages with the stories printed in long columns. Meg glanced at the headlines. There was an article about John A. Macdonald, a report on people arrested for drunkenness and a big story about a house break-in on Shuter Street.

Bud and Paddy were ahead of them on the street and were beginning to pick up a chant. "*Globe*! Get your *Globe* here! Hot off the presses. Burglaries on Shuter Street. More drunks arrested. Get your *Globe* here!" Already the boys had made a couple of sales.

They were starting to head north on Yonge Street when Paddy stopped to let Jamie and Meg catch up. "You have to shout out the news," he explained. "Bud and I have a corner over on Bay Street. You're going to have to find a place to stand. Just shout out the headlines. You'll be all right. We'll meet you back at the *Globe* building." Then the two boys took off up the street at a sprint, anxious to get on with the business of making money.

"Where should we go, Meg?"

"I don't know. Maybe we should just head up Yonge. It looks busy."

A group of men in business suits were coming down the street. Jamie held up the paper showing the headlines and shouted, "*Globe*! Get your *Globe* here! Robberies on Shuter Street. Lots of drunkenness. Get your *Globe* here!" The boy felt slightly foolish, but it seemed to work. A couple of men thrust big copper coins into his hand and took a paper. When he felt the money jangling in his pocket he smiled. He was going to like this.

Meg went down the other side of the street and the two picked up the chant. By the time they got to Queen Street they had sold two more papers each.

It was around six-thirty in the morning now and already the sun was up in a clear blue sky. It was going to be a beautiful day. As they walked along the wooden sidewalk they passed fashionable shops of every description, but dust covered everything. Yonge Street was unpaved and every time a wagon passed, the horses and wheels kicked up dust.

They passed newsboys at every corner as they went north, but when they got to the corner of Queen it was deserted. It seemed like a good spot with lots of traffic and people on foot coming from all directions. Jamie stood on one corner and his sister on the other, shouting out their patter in loud voices.

"*Globe*! Get your *Globe* here. Robberies on Shuter Street. The *Globe*. Hot off the presses."

There was lots of business. The papers were going out fast and change swelled their pockets. Most of the sales were to people walking, but a couple of men leaned out of their carriage windows to buy papers. There was even a well-dressed man riding a bicycle with a big front wheel who stopped, bought a paper, thrust it into his coat and then awkwardly climbed back on the tall vehicle. For a moment he tottered dangerously, then picked up speed and peddled down the street.

Jamie was so preoccupied making sales that he didn't see Stinger arrive.

"What are you doin' on my corner?" the muscular boy demanded. He had two stacks of papers under each arm.

"Your corner?"

"Yes, my corner! Queen and Yonge is my corner and nobody sells here. I've had it from you, kid. I'm going to bust your head open." Stinger put his papers down and started to go after Jamie.

"I didn't know. We're new here."

"You're going to be eatin' dirt." His arms were long, his chest powerful, and the look on his face was mean.

Jamie backed up. "I'm leaving. I didn't know it was your corner. I'm sorry." Then he turned and hurriedly crossed the street.

"It's Stinger's corner," he explained to Meg.

"Maybe it won't be as easy to get rid of these papers as it looked. We've still got a lot to sell if we're going to make any money."

The two of them continued to walk north, calling out the name of the paper and the headlines in loud voices. A horse car came down Yonge Street carrying people to work. When it stopped a number of people got off and bought papers from Meg.

Up the street they met a boy they had seen in the *Globe* office. He suggested they take the next north-bound horse car and go up to the town of Yorkville. A few minutes later one came lumbering along and they climbed aboard.

After they had paid the fare they sold a couple of copies to passengers and sat down. Between the two of them they still had over fifty papers left.

"We could almost walk faster than this horse can pull us. Maybe we should get out and sell as we go," said Jamie.

But they stayed aboard the car and watched the passing scene through the windows. Shops lined the streets until they crossed College. After that there was a series of attached houses built up to the boardwalk. Almost every corner had a tavern with colourful signs hanging over the street, and churches were everywhere, their spires rising high above the squat surrounding houses.

The horse-drawn car crossed Bloor Street, and the conductor announced that they were at the Yorkville terminus. Meg and Jamie scrambled out, eager to sell their remaining stack of papers.

Groups of prosperous-looking men were standing at the terminus waiting for the car to circle around and begin heading down Yonge Street again. Jamie and Meg hurried over and sold at least a dozen papers in short order. It was a great spot.

But they were at the stop for less than half an hour when another couple of newsboys showed up and claimed it as their territory. Again they were forced to move. They walked north on Yonge, past the toll gate where a uniformed official collected fees from each passing wagon and coach. Then they stood outside the Red Lion Inn, a white, rough-cast establishment, for a few minutes, but they made only an occasional sale.

"We've still got close to thirty papers, and it's already eight o'clock," sighed Jamie.

It was one of the boys selling at the horse car terminus who suggested they go over to the university. They walked west along Bloor, shouting their chants as they went and making a few sales. At Taddle Creek they cut down to McCaul's Pond and through the grassed, park-like area until they got to University College.

There they met serious-looking students in their early twenties who seemed anxious to avoid the profane world the newspaper portrayed. One of them read the headlines with concern. "More drunkenness. Where will it all end?"

But finally the problem did end for Meg and Jamie. By nine-thirty they had sold all of their papers and their pockets were filled with coins.

CHAPTER 3

IT was ten o'clock before they got back to the *Globe* building. There they found a group of newsboys sitting in a grassed area warming themselves in the bright sunshine. Bud and Paddy were among them, but at the centre was Stinger.

"Did you see that Moffat this mornin'?" the big boy said loudly. Stinger had his shirt off, showing off his powerful chest and arms. "He don't know what's goin' on in this city. I tell you them coppers in this town are stupid. Why, I could scoff the bell out of the Church Street Cathedral and no one would be the wiser."

Jamie sat beside Bud and Paddy and listened to Stinger's performance while Meg gathered her legs under her and began studying the Help Wanted column in the newspaper that she had saved. There were not many jobs listed, but she scanned the list carefully. A foundry wanted a skilled sheet metal worker, there was an ad for an experienced typesetter to work in a small print shop and several notices asking for domestic help. Meg couldn't stand the idea of doing dishes and laundry all day for someone else at dirt-poor wages.

The only job that looked at all promising was working in a warehouse. She read the advertisement several times. They would probably want a man, but there was no hint of that in the notice. Maybe they would take her. It was worth a try.

When she glanced up she saw her brother sitting with the other boys, listening to the boastful banter that was going on. He looked completely at home, as if he had always been a part of the group.

Stinger was holding forth. "We should go down to that Upper Canada College place there to get the toffs when they're on their way home from school. What with their suits all pressed and tidy and their ties just right they need a good toss in the mud just to make them human. Anyone want to take them on with me?"

There were a lot of smiles but no one volunteered. All the boys seemed to like to hear Stinger's tough talk, but they weren't about to follow him on a crazy adventure that would land them in trouble.

"Jamie … " Meg called. When he looked up she motioned him to come over. Paddy and Bud came with him. "What are you going to do for the rest of the day?"

He shrugged. "I don't know."

"We usually go shoe shinin' around lunch time," Paddy explained. "Then after that we sell the evening papers."

"I'm going off to try and get a job," said Meg. "You should come with me."

"Aw, Meg. Don't you think I can stay with the boys?"

"We've got to look for good jobs. We can't sell newspapers all our lives."

Jamie looked at his new friends for a moment. They seemed relaxed and happy. Just to hang about on the streets and do nothing was so appealing to him. "Why can't I sell newspapers for awhile, Meg?"

The girl studied her brother. He looked small and vulnerable. Perhaps she should let him work with the other boys.

"He can stay with us," said Paddy. "We'll show him the ropes."

"Well … would you like that, Jamie?"

"Yeah, sure," he smiled. "I'll be safe enough, Meg. You can trust me."

"All right, then."

They agreed to meet back at their lodgings at three in the afternoon, and Meg went off in search of a full-time job. The boys went back to sitting on the grass listening to Stinger for awhile. In time the others drifted away, and then there were just the three of them.

Jamie loved the easy familiarity of the boys. He had been cooped up in a factory for so long that he had almost forgotten what it was like to be carefree and have a good time.

"Where's your family?" Jamie asked.

"We're family to each other," answered Paddy.

"But I mean your mother and father?"

"My parents left me in an orphanage," explained Paddy. "I couldn't stand it anymore so I just ran away. Bud — his father used to drink so much that he figured he was better off on his own."

"Where do you live?"

Bud looked around to make sure no one was listening. "Don't tell anyone, but we've got a hideout."

"Where?"

"You shouldn't have told," said Paddy.

"Doesn't matter. Jamie's a good friend. Winter was hard on us," Bud explained. "We had to sleep in doorways and sometimes went hungry. But now we got ourselves a real hideout over on Toronto Island. We've got a boat and everything. It's perfect. Nobody knows about it, but we're so close to the city that we can get here in twenty minutes."

"A real hideout?" Jamie was impressed. "Can I see it sometime?"

"Maybe," said Paddy, getting to his feet. "Come on. If we're going to make any money today we've got to get moving."

The *Globe* had a place where the news sellers could store their gear, and that was where the boys kept their shoeshine outfit. The box was a homemade wooden affair with a sliding lid and a stand on the top for the customer to place his foot. Inside was boot black polish, a pair of brushes and a soft rag for buffing. Bud slung the leather strap of the box over his shoulder and they headed off.

They walked over to Yonge Street and saw a wagon heading south. With a quick dash the two boys darted out and hitched a ride by scrambling onto the back bumper. Bud waved frantically at Jamie and he ran to join them. The horse trotted down the street unaware of the added baggage.

"Never walk when you can take a ride like this," whispered Paddy.

"Yeah, and never pay the horse car fare unless you have to." They were spotted by several people sitting on the back of the wagon. Their obvious disapproval only made the boys feel more defiant. At Front Street a policeman shouted at them. The three boys jumped off, giggling to themselves, and ran along the street until they were certain the officer was not following.

They headed over to the Queen's Hotel on Front Street, the big fancy establishment Jamie and Meg had seen the day before. It was a magnificent, well-kept place with a private garden and large fountain surrounded by a wrought-iron fence. As they came up to the pillared entrance of the hotel they found that Stinger was already there with his box over his shoulder.

"Get lost!" he said in a snarl. "I'm here first."

"There's enough trade for us all," Paddy replied.

Just then a frock-coated gentleman with a top hat and walking stick came out of the hotel. "Want a shoe shine?" Bud asked and the man agreed.

"That could have been my customer," Stinger whispered, annoyed. "You scooped him from me."

"We can all work here," answered Jamie.

Just then another man came out of the hotel. Stinger got him as a customer and the argument was forgotten. Business was brisk and the boys took turns shining shoes and sharing the money.

They had been there about an hour when Murphy came striding down the street with another man of about twenty-five. They made an odd pair. Murphy was tall with a ruddy face, long sideburns, a suit, bowler hat and his ever-present cigar glowing in his mouth. The man with him was short with powerful shoulders and a square clean-shaven face that was reddish and speckled with freckles. He wore an open-necked shirt and fancy waistcoat without a jacket.

Murphy spotted Jamie and greeted him with his loud voice that suggested he had been drinking too much. "Well, if it isn't me little half-pint farthin', Jamie Bains. Scrapin' out a livin' as a boot black on the streets of Toronto."

"Would you like a shoe shine, Mr. Murphy?" asked Jamie feebly.

"And why not? There's money in me pocket and a fair chance to make a fortune in this fine city." He turned to the younger man who was with him. "Have yourself a shoe shine, there, Darnby, me boy. The treat's on me. It's just a little somethin' to celebrate our new business arrangement."

"Suppose I don't mind if I do. It's time to get that circus mud off these shoes and start my new life." Darnby spoke with a broad Canadian accent that had a hint of country in it.

Jamie set the box on the sidewalk and took out the equipment. Murphy put his foot up on the rest, and the boy began slathering the boot with polish. Darnby stood beside him and his boots were polished by Stinger.

Murphy was in an expansive mood. "See this lad, here, Darnby. Jamie Bains is his name. Used to work for me at Lachine Mill in Montreal, but look at him now. A street boy up to no good. I always figured him and that sister of his would come to a bad end." He puffed on his cigar until it glowed red. There was the smell of whisky about him.

"This is honest work, sir," Jamie replied defensively.

"Honest? Not if I know the street boys in this town." Darnby laughed. "They're worse than a city full of vagabonds. They say the street kids in Toronto are so fast you never know your pocket's been picked till you're back home again." The man talked like a huckster out to sell tickets on a side show.

Jamie worked away at the boot without saying a word. There was nothing he liked about Murphy, and his friend seemed little better. But the other boys had come closer to hear the extravagant chatter of the two men.

Murphy had pushed his hat to the back of his head and stood with his arms folded across his ample stomach as his shoes were being polished. Darnby had hooked his thumbs into his waistcoat and talked away as if he didn't have a care in the world.

"It's business for myself that I'm going into," Murphy announced. "Buying and selling things. There's a handsome profit in that." He paused for a moment, studying Stinger, Paddy and Bud. A smile crept over his whiskered face. "What do you think, Darnby? I'd wager my last dollar that these boys have something to sell."

"I suppose, Murphy. Street boys like this always have a little merchandise. Isn't that right?"

Stinger looked around guiltily. "Might have."

Darnby smiled and then glanced meaningfully at Murphy. "What's your name, kid?"

"Stinger."

"Stinger, is it?" And he gave a sharp laugh. "I bet you've learned to sting the population of this here good city."

"I get by."

The Irishman leaned back. "Well, now, my little friends. If it's a business partner that you're lookin' for, then I think you have found it in Darnby and yours truly, John Murphy. The two of us have a good sense for profit and that's the truth."

"What kind of profit?" asked Stinger suspiciously.

"Give me your other foot, Mr. Murphy," Jamie said. He felt very uncomfortable and found himself working furiously to get the boots finished.

"Ah, me lad, there's only one kind of profit, and that's lots of it," said Murphy. "I'm interested in money. That's the only thing that keeps hunger from the door. There was a day when I starved like you young tykes. I lived through the Irish famine with nothin' to eat but thin soup made out of nettles. I saw me family die around me and grown men fight over crusts of bread. I swore it was never going to happen to me again."

Jamie slathered the boot polish on as fast as he could go, but the conversation continued without a pause.

Darnby leaned forward. "Look at these four young boys here, Murphy. Hain't it a cryin' shame? Starvin' all the time and no one cares. The people in this town would let 'em freeze in the winter and sleep out on the beaches in the summer. They pretend that they're moral and upright, but they're only concerned about what's in their pockets."

"So what can we do?" asked Paddy innocently.

"It's money, my friend. Everyone needs money." Darnby had a smile on his red freckled face. "When you see the rich comin' down the street all decked out in their fine clothes, do you ever think that maybe it's not fair that they've got silver and gold jangling in their pockets while you've got nothin' but a hungry belly and cold lodgings in some dirty boarding house? Do you ever think of that?"

"But what can you do about it?" asked Paddy.

"It's not up to me. Fellers like you have to help themselves. You've got to be strong minded and say you don't intend to be livin' in poverty again. Maybe I can help a little, but you've got to do most of it."

Jamie had the brushes out now, and he was polishing away at Murphy's shoes as hard as he could go.

"You see," continued Darnby, "I think that we should share the wealth. But since nobody's there to give the poor a hand then I believe fellers like ourselves will just have to do it alone."

"How?" said Stinger intently.

"It's take from the rich and give to the poor. Social justice, that's what I call it. And there hain't none more poor than you street boys."

Stinger looked around to make sure no one was listening. "You mean like … "

Darnby was nodding, his face flushed a deep red. "You're gettin' the idea. I think we could enter into a profitable partnership. It would be done in the name of social justice, of course. But you boys have your ways of operating, and we have — how shall I call it — our business connections. I think we could help each other."

Jamie was polishing now, furiously whipping the cloth over the shoe until the leather gleamed a deep black.

"Well, I don't know," Stinger was saying. "It seems to me that I'm doin' all right by myself."

"Are you sure you get the best possible prices?" asked Darnby.

Now Jamie stood up. "I'm done, Mr. Murphy."

The big man studied his gleaming shoes. "Well, me boy, it seems like you've learned some useful trade since you've come to this upright city." He reached into his pocket, still puffing on his cigar, extracted a ten cent piece and gave it to Jamie.

When Stinger had finished, Darnby reached into his pocket and with a great flourish extracted a gleaming twenty-five cent piece. Then with a flip of his thumb the coin was spun high in the air. Just as Stinger was about to catch it, Darnby snatched it in mid flight.

"Got to be fast to make it in this world," he said with a laugh. Now he held up both of his hands. They were empty. "Where did it go? Oh, there it is." And he reached up to snatch the coin from behind Bud's ear.

"How did you do that?" asked the young boy, amazed.

"She's all in the art of the hands, boys." Now Darnby was rolling the coin along his knuckles so quickly it seemed alive. With a final flourish he flipped the twenty-five cent piece up in the air towards Stinger. When it came down the boy fumbled and dropped it.

"You fellers think it over," Darnby announced casually. "You need money to keep hunger from the door, and we're just the ones to make it possible. Murphy and I are staying in a small tavern called the Boar's Head down at the bottom of Jarvis Street near the wharves. You think good and hard about it and then we'll be talkin' again."

Murphy puffed a big cloud of smoke from his cigar, and then the two men swaggered down the street towards Yonge, as carefree as anyone out for a stroll on a warm summer day.

CHAPTER 4

NOT long after they had arrived in Toronto, Jamie and Meg had fallen into a new pattern. Meg started a job as a stock clerk's helper at a warehouse down on Front Street, working every day from six-thirty in the morning to six at night, five-and-a-half days a week, while Jamie became completely absorbed into the life of the street boys.

Already he looked like them. His hair was lighter and his skin had taken on a healthy tone from spending hours in the sun. He became scruffy and unkempt. A permanent grime dirtied his hands, the shirt he wore sprouted tears, buttons were lost, and his pants had a rip at the knee.

Meg wondered about the hours her brother spent with his friends hanging out on street corners as they told each other stories in the swaggering tone they all affected. She tried to talk him into looking for another job and reminded him that they needed to save money to send home to their mother, but it didn't do any good. He wasn't interested in looking for another job, and now that his clothes were such a shambles, who would hire him?

Jamie was happy with his new life. After the grinding discipline of the Montreal factory this casual way of living suited him just fine. As the first heat wave of summer came, and the hot humidity made the streets radiate with warmth, he and the other newsboys found every possible excuse to avoid work.

One hot day, after selling a hundred copies of the *Globe*, he went back to the newspaper building and found Bud and Paddy along with a group of others on their favourite spot of grass in the yard.

"Want to go out to our hideout today?" Paddy whispered so the others wouldn't hear. "Bud and I are going to take the rest of the day off and go swimming."

Jamie's face brightened. "Sure sounds great. When do we go?"

"We were just waiting for you. Come on."

As they got to their feet, Stinger, who was the centre of another clique of boys, also stood up. "Hey, where are you goin'?" He came over and stood in front of them, his hands on his hips.

"We're just headin' down to the harbour to look around," Paddy answered cautiously.

"I hear you got a skiff. Goin' for a ride over to your place on the island?"

"Yeah … well, maybe."

"Good. I'll come along, too."

Paddy looked at Bud and then at Jamie. Finally he nodded and said flatly, "All right, Stinger. Get your stuff."

It promised to be a perfect day. The sun was only part way up but already it spread a sweltering heat among the close-set buildings of the city. Jamie felt a growing excitement. Just to be on his own — free and with no responsibilities — felt great.

Bud led the way along King Street to Church, down to Front Street and over to the St. Lawrence Market, a reddish brick building with arched windows in the front and a clock tower.

The boys cut through the building, dawdling to look at the goods displayed in the stalls. There were children's toys and knick-knacks, cheap jewellery, perfume, candies and second-hand books. In the back of the building were butchers' stalls and farmers' wagons laden with meats, jugs of milk, cream and cheese. Vegetable stalls had tables filled with potatoes, carrots, apples and red strawberries, the first of the season. Jamie got hungry just looking at everything. If only they had a little money, what a feast they could have.

The four boys came out of the back of the building, crossed Jarvis Street and headed down towards the harbour.

"Have an apple?" said Stinger, pulling a number of juicy ones from under his shirt.

"Where'd you get them?" Jamie asked.

"Got to be quick of hand to survive in this town." And the boy laughed.

Jamie felt an unease in the pit of his stomach, but he ate the apple like the others and joined in the easy banter.

"That's where Darnby and Murphy are staying," said Paddy, pointing to the tavern called the Boar's Head tucked up an alley among some warehouses and small factories. "Want to visit them?"

"Not me," said Jamie. "I've seen enough of Murphy."

"I went over and met that Darnby guy," added Stinger. "He's got a good deal for us."

"I like Darnby," said Bud. "He's real neat the way he can make that quarter disappear."

They crossed over the railway line and walked along the waterfront next to the docks. An old side-wheeler was taking on a load of grain at Beard's Wharf, and they could see a group of burly stevedores unloading coal from the hold of a three-masted schooner. Wagons of all descriptions were lined up waiting for their loads, and big stacks of barrels and heavy crates were piled high on the wharves.

They went east until they came to a place with a small painted sign saying Taylor's Wharf. It was a wood-planked affair where small boats were tied up. At the end of the dock Bud scrambled down a ladder and manoeuvred a skiff around until the four of them could climb down into it. Then, with Paddy at the oars, they glided out into the harbour.

Once on the water the scene opened up around them. The yellow sun gleaming on the surface made them squint from the glare. It was scalding hot on the boys' chests and arms, and soon they were stripping off shirts, shoes and socks. But the farther they went into the harbour the more the water cooled the air. A slight breeze stirred the surface and ruffled their hair.

Jamie sat at the bow, his hand dangling in the cool water. They passed two schooners riding gently at anchor, with their sails hanging slack in the breeze. Out farther were rowboats and sailing vessels of every description. A small steamboat passed them and their skiff rocked up and down in its wake.

Gradually they rowed across the harbour, and the islands of Toronto drew closer. They looked like a long spit of sand stretching out from shore with a channel cut through its eastern section. To the west Jamie could see a few buildings and a tall lighthouse standing prominently on the shore, but the eastern part of the islands, where they were headed, was a dense green jungle of trees. Behind them was the city with its busy harbour but before them lay a deserted maze of lagoons, sand bars and scattered miniature islands. As they drew closer, the place seemed to enclose them into its own private world of sand, water, trees and sky.

"Get ready now," Paddy said suddenly. "We're coming into shore."

The boat was gliding onto a golden sand beach. Big weeping willow trees overhung the water with their long dangling leaves drooping almost to the surface. Beyond the narrow beach there was a low embankment.

Jamie rolled up his pants and when the bottom of the skiff scraped the sand, he climbed over the side into the cool, ankle-deep water and began pulling the boat ashore.

"We want to take her in behind that log." Paddy pointed with an oar. "There's a little place where we can hide the boat."

"Where's the camp?" Jamie asked.

"You'll see," Bud answered with a smile.

The four boys got out of the skiff and manoeuvred it behind the log until it was completely hidden from view.

"We're squatters," Paddy explained. "If the police were to find us we'd be rousted out real quick."

They found the camp behind the embankment nestled under the willow branches. The boys had made a lean-to out of heavy canvas stretched across long poles. Their bed of reeds and grass was covered with heavy woollen blankets. To the front of the lean-to were the blackened remains of a fire with two cooking pots propped up on rocks.

The hideout was just perfect, Jamie thought. No one could see them nestled in among the trees, but they could sit and look out across the bay and see the city.

He went and stood on the narrow beach, letting the sun warm his body. Not far away was the Eastern Gap leading out to the lake, and as he stood there a magnificent white riverboat, its side-wheels churning, and belching thick black smoke from its tall stack, entered the harbour. To the west he could see three racing sailboats running before the light breeze. There were scullers practising and boys fishing from skiffs. Across the water lay the city, quiet and subdued from this distance.

"I tell you Darnby's got the answer," Jamie heard Stinger say as the others came to join him on the beach. "He says we're gonna make big profits."

"But, Stinger, we could get caught. If Bud and I go back before that judge he's going to send us away to the reformatory for sure."

"Aw, them coppers can't catch nobody. Detective Moffat's stupid. He couldn't catch an apple thief if he scoffed a barrel right before his eyes."

Jamie frowned. What were the boys talking about?

"You don't understand," Stinger continued. "Darnby's got it all figured out."

Paddy looked uneasy. "I don't know. Bud and I are doin' all right. We got this place … "

"But last winter you almost starved. Remember? I seen you out sleeping in alleyways and beggin' for food. It's not right. People should share their wealth. That's what Darnby says, but they just let us starve so we gotta look after ourselves."

"I don't know."

"Look, it's all set up. Now that we've got this hideout it's perfect. Them coppers will be searchin' high and low all over the city and we'll be out here on the island just enjoying ourselves safe as a church."

Jamie threw stones into the water and felt the warm sun on his back as he listened. What had Darnby and Stinger cooked up between them?

"Let's do something," said Paddy suddenly, changing the subject. "Now that we've taken the day off we should enjoy it."

"I'd like to go for a swim," said Bud.

"Too cold in the harbour. Let's take the boat up the Don River to the water hole."

Within moments they had hauled their skiff out of its hiding place and set off across the water again. This time Jamie took the oars, and he bent into the work with pleasure. Soon he had developed an easy rhythm, pulling on the oars with his back and legs and using the full extent of his arms. The small skiff glided quickly along the calm water.

"You're pretty good on them oars, there, Jamie," Stinger said, laughing.

Jamie rowed across the bay. Then, at Paddy's directions, they rounded a long jetty, passing the wharf of Gooderham and Worts Distillery. It was then that the boy looked up and saw the ominous grey-stoned prison.

But soon they entered the mouth of the Don. At first the river water was swampy with reeds crowding the bank and long brown cat-tails swaying in the light breeze. The water was a smelly, sluggish stream with garbage and filth littering the shore. The boat slid under the railway bridge, past the packing house and another couple of bridges. By then the river, running over a gravel and sand bed, was as clean as sunshine.

They found themselves in a gently sloping valley with meadow lands rolling gracefully down to the river bed. Tall elm trees with their long drooping branches were spotted in the fields, and along the ridges were dark pine trees. In one field there were cows. In another a herd of grazing sheep. The boys passed turtles and black snakes sunning themselves on the river bank and logs.

"Look," said Stinger, pointing to a huge fortress-like building high up on the east bank. "There's the new Don Jail. The other place just wasn't big enough for all the people wantin' to get into it."

Jamie looked at Stinger sharply. "How do know?"

But Stinger just laughed. Before Jamie could say any more, the skiff rounded a bend and startled a muskrat chewing on some reeds up on the bank. In a panic the small animal plunged into the water and disappeared. Jamie let the skiff drift as they looked for him. They had almost given up when the muskrat suddenly poked his nose above the surface, spotted them watching and disappeared again, this time for good.

Now the river was faster. In a couple of places the boys had to get out of their boat and haul it through rapid water. In another spot the river spread out over a long shallow bar, and they had to wade, ankle deep, until they were in the dark still water again.

"There's Castle Frank," said Bud, pointing to a building standing on a high bank to the west. "Bloor Street's just up a ways. There's a great water hole around the next bend."

It was a beautiful spot. The east bank was a low, grassed meadow with a couple of big elm trees. The opposite side rose ten feet or more out of the water, making a table-like grassy area overlooking the pool. The water was so clean they could see right down to the bottom. As they glided into shore they spotted sunfish hiding in among the reeds.

The skiff slid easily onto a sandy bar, and the boys piled out. "Let's go!" Bud shouted excitedly. "Last one in's gonna be a jailbird!"

tripped off their clothes as fast as they
ent flying into the bushes, pants were

"That's not fair," Paddy said. "You guys got no belts." He fumbled with a rope he had tied around his waist.

Bud was first. As soon as he was naked the small boy ran for the water and leapt in feet first, making a huge shower. Stinger was in next and then Paddy. Jamie was last of all. He ran to the water's edge and paused for a moment. The others splashed him, shouting and laughing as he tried to dodge the water. Then he leapt out, holding his nose as he flopped, backside first, into the pool. The water closed over him in a great rush. For just an instant it was bitingly cold, but then felt refreshingly cool.

As he came to the surface the boys were laughing and shouting to each other. Paddy splashed water, sending up showers, while Bud swam underwater like a fish, grabbing at feet. They had races to the end of the pool, and then saw how long they could stay underwater.

Paddy swam to the west bank and found a way to climb up the steep cliff that rose out of the water. Once he was on the embankment he ran, leaping off the high bank, screaming in excitement. Then the others followed. Over and over they made wild, running jumps, until finally they just didn't have any more strength.

They swam for what seemed like hours and then climbed up the bank beside the boat and lay down in the soft grass, letting the sun bake their naked bodies. Lazily they whiled away the afternoon telling stories and repeating old jokes.

Jamie found a special magic about the place. The sun hung high, shining out of a clear blue sky, slanting

through the tall trees to give a bright green richness to
the valley and make the water gleam and dance as the
surface caught the light.

The place was perfect, except for Stinger. The older
boy remained remote from the others — a brooding
blight on the warm glow of the day. It was more than a
dislike that Jamie felt. It was a growing fear of Stinger
that left him with a nagging uneasiness.

Finally, the sun dipped behind the trees that stood
high up on the hill behind Castle Frank, and they knew
it was time to go. The boys dressed, got into their skiff
and leisurely rowed downstream, letting the current do
most of the work. When they got to the Queen Street
bridge Bud nosed the boat into shore. Jamie and Stinger
climbed out. Paddy and Bud headed down river towards
the bay and their island hideout while the other two
climbed up the bank and began walking into the city.

It was as they were going along King Street that
Stinger said suddenly, "You up for a little fun, Jamie?"

"Fun? What do you mean?"

They were walking past run-down houses built
close to the street. Children were everywhere. Carts
pulled by big horses went trotting by or stood idle as
drivers made deliveries. A policeman in his blue
uniform, tall helmet, and holding a long black night
stick, stood on a corner as they walked past.

"Don't know about you, Jamie. Been watchin', but
I'm not sure you're really one of us."

"Sure I am."

A bread wagon with a closed cart was standing in the middle of the block. The driver was nowhere in sight.

"Got to have nerves of steel to be part of our gang," said Stinger with a smile. Now he skipped forward, almost dancing in excitement. "Watch this."

With a quick dash Stinger was at the bread wagon, had the back door open and came out with a loaf of sweet rolls with white frosting over the top. In a flash he had handed it to Jamie and closed the cart door.

"Hey! Come back here with that!" came a shriek from the bread man across the street. "Thief! You're stealing! Come back here!"

Jamie and Stinger began to move. The older boy, a big smile on his face, ran quickly. Out of panic Jamie followed. He carried the sticky rolls in both hands, uncertain what to do with them. The policeman behind them on the corner heard the commotion and began to follow.

The bread man had put down his wicker basket and was running after them, shouting at them to stop. But now the policeman was sprinting, holding his night stick out in front of him. In a few strides he had passed the delivery man and was gaining on the boys.

Stinger was laughing. "Split up," he shouted and then suddenly veered north on Parliament Street, running hard. In a moment he had disappeared.

Jamie was in a panic. He had to get away, but he continued to clutch the sweet rolls, his fingers digging into the sticky frosting. He ran with every ounce of strength in his legs.

West on Queen he went, almost bumping into an old man and bursting through a group of children playing hopscotch. He glanced back. The policeman was running hard. Could he escape?

At the next corner he swung left and ran across the street, darting dangerously in front of a horse and cart. He spotted an alleyway and sprinted down it as hard as he could go.

He glanced down at the rolls in his hands. What should he do with them? If the policeman caught him with the goods it would be jail for sure. Without slowing his pace he tossed them over a board fence and ran even harder.

As he got to the end of the alley he heard the policeman shouting, "Come back here, boy! We know who you are! We'll get you!"

But Jamie sped through a maze of streets and back alleys and was gone.

CHAPTER 5

THAT evening Jamie sat on his bed brooding as he watched Meg prepare their supper. Images swirled through his mind: Stinger raiding the bakery truck, the fat bread man shouting "thief" at the top of his voice and the policeman chasing him. The events still seemed so vivid that fear and panic seized him once again.

Meg suddenly put down the knife she was using and looked at her brother with annoyance. "Can't you give me some help, Jamie?" She studied him for a moment. "What's bothering you?"

"Nothing," he shrugged as he got up to help her.

"Are you sure?" Meg looked at him closely.

"Nothing's wrong." But the anxiety had turned to a sick feeling in his stomach.

"I don't like you selling newspapers." She went back to cutting their dried cheese into thick slices. "Why don't you look for another job?"

"But there is no other work, and selling newspapers is a lot better than working in a factory where you don't even get to go outside."

Meg pushed back a wisp of blond hair that had come loose from her bun. "But we've got to send money back to mother, and you can't save anything on the money you make."

"Leave me alone, Meg. You're always bossing me around," Jamie said, annoyed. Where was a twelve-year-old boy like himself going to find a job when grown men were begging for work? And anyway, he liked selling newspapers.

By the time they sat down to eat it was dark in their dingy room. Meg lit a candle and the flame gave off a yellowish, dancing light that did little to drive back the shadows. Their meagre supper of cheese, milk and bread was eaten in silence.

It was as they were clearing the table that there were three sharp knocks at the door. Jamie froze. Meg was halfway to the door when the heavy pounding came again. "Who is it?" she asked timidly.

"Police! Open up!"

As the door swung open the light of the candle revealed a tall, square-shouldered young policeman in full blue uniform and tall helmet. Beside him was Detective Moffat. Jamie could see the shape of his bowler hat perched on the back of his head. His thumbs were hooked into his waistcoat pockets.

"You Jamie Bains?" Moffat asked grimly.

Jamie was riveted to his spot. His hands gripped the back of a chair.

"What is it?" Meg asked. "What do you want with Jamie?"

"Just a little truth. Some good old-fashioned honesty." The policeman looked around the room as if he was memorizing every detail.

"Did he do anything wrong?"

"Maybe." The detective took one of the hard-backed chairs, turned it around and sat on it backwards, straddling the chair with both legs. He studied the boy in the flickering light of the candle for what seemed like a long time before asking, "Where were you late this afternoon?"

Jamie swallowed hard. His heart was beating so loudly he was sure Moffat could hear it. "I was ... I was out with some friends."

"Where?"

"We went swimming up the Don River."

"Then what did you do?"

"Came home."

"Were you with Stinger when you came home?" Moffat's eyes never left the boy.

Jamie glanced nervously at his sister. She looked shocked. "Ah ... yes, sir."

Slowly the policeman got to his feet. His look was dark and foreboding. "You stole from the bread truck. Isn't that right, Jamie?"

The boy looked from the detective to the uniformed policeman guarding the door, to his sister and back to Moffat again. They were all waiting expectantly. "No, sir, I didn't do it. I didn't steal."

Moffat smiled cynically. Then he walked across the room and looked out the window for a moment. When he looked back his mouth was set in a hard scowl. "You're innocent. Is that what you're telling me?"

"I didn't do anything, sir."

"That's not what our constable says, and we've got a bread man who swears that you stole some sweet rolls out of his wagon."

"It isn't true, sir. Really it isn't."

The policeman walked slowly across the room and stood towering over him. "Are you saying that they are lying?"

"No, sir." There was a catch in his voice.

"Then tell me what happened."

The boy swallowed hard. He looked up and found Meg staring at him. "We were coming up the street, sir. The bread wagon was there … " He paused, breathing heavily. Could he really tell them everything that had happened? What if Stinger found out?

"And then what happened?"

Jamie looked at his sister and back at the detective. His stomach was twisted into a knot.

"Tell us what happened!" Meg insisted.

The boy swallowed hard. "The bread man saw us and we started running, and … and then the policeman chased us."

Moffat leaned across the table. "Is that all that happened?"

"Yes, sir. We ran 'cause we got scared. We ran and ran until we got away."

"That's not how I heard the story. My information is that Stinger took some sweet rolls from the cart, but you took them from him and ran away."

"No, sir. It's not the way it happened." Now he was breathing so hard he was almost panting.

Suddenly Meg broke in. "Why didn't you tell me this, Jamie?"

"But I didn't take the rolls, Meg."

"That's not the way Stinger tells the story," the policeman said. "He blamed it all on you."

"He did?"

"How do you think I got your name?"

"Stinger told you?"

"You're surprised?" the detective said sarcastically. "Did you think there was honour between thieves?"

Jamie opened his mouth and then closed it again. He was too shocked to speak.

"It doesn't look good for you, boy. I think I'll have to take you down to the police station until I get some truth out of you."

"But, sir. I didn't want to do it. I just ran!"

"Stinger said it was your idea all along." The detective pushed his hat to the back of his head and put his fists on his hips. He was towering over the boy. "I think some time in the cells might clear your head. Then we can get at the truth."

"But I am telling the truth." Jamie was beginning to feel desperate now. Tears were gathering in his eyes.

Moffat shook his head. "Trouble. That's what I see here. Anyone who runs with someone like Stinger is headed for serious trouble. You're the kind of boy who'll spend half your life in jail and the other half getting into trouble unless you straighten out now."

The bleak prediction made tears roll down Jamie's face. He began to sob.

The detective turned away and began looking through their room. He opened cupboard doors, examined their empty shelves and then looked through the few worn pieces of clothing that hung on nails.

Meg looked desperate. She was supposed to be responsible for her brother. What would her mother say when she found out that Jamie had been stealing? "I'm willing to pay for whatever was taken, Mr. Moffat, sir," she said.

The detective turned and looked at the girl as Meg took out her change purse and counted out big pennies onto the table. "I'll pay for everything."

"That may satisfy the baker, but what should I do about the boy?"

"I won't do it again, sir. I promise," Jamie pleaded as he tried to wipe his face dry.

"He'll stay honest, sir. I give my word on that."

The policeman studied them both for what seemed like a long time and then he nodded. "All right, Jamie, I'll give you a break just this one time, but if it ever happens again we're going to lock you up and throw away the keys. Do you understand?"

"Yes, sir. I understand."

After his speech the policeman carefully collected enough pennies off the table to pay for the sweet rolls and with a curt nod to his partner the two of them were out the door and gone.

That evening Meg and Jamie talked about what had happened until there was no more to say. The boy made promises. He would stay away from Stinger and look for a steady job. Above all he declared that his days of crime were over. When Meg was satisfied that he meant it they went to bed.

But the next morning things felt different. Jamie arrived early at the *Globe* office. Stinger was already in the line and the bigger boy strode across the room to him. He wore a strange smile on his face.

"Why did you tell the police?" Jamie whispered as he glanced about to see if anyone was listening.

"I didn't tell nobody nothin'."

"Detective Moffat came by our lodgings last night. He said that you told him … "

"Listen, kid. Don't listen to what none of them coppers say. They're always tellin' lies."

"How else would they know that I was involved if you didn't tell them?"

"Forget about that. Forget it. We got better things to do." Then Stinger looked around suspiciously. He crouched forward to whisper. "We've got to talk. You and me and Bud and Paddy. We've got to make our plans."

"What sort of plans?"

"Can't say now. Meet me out in the yard after you sell your papers."

Jamie wanted to ask what it was all about, but Stinger wouldn't wait. "In the yard after you sell your papers," he repeated and then went back to take his place in line.

That uneasy feeling came back to Jamie. It was just as well that Meg wasn't there to see him talk with Stinger. He wished that Bud and Paddy would arrive so he could talk things over with them, but they didn't come in until after the pressmen were counting out the newspapers. There was nothing to do but take his papers and get out on the street to sell them. He would worry about Stinger later.

Jamie had a good morning. A few days before he had managed to get the corner of Front and Bay streets, close by the Jacques and Hay furniture factory, to sell his papers. Already he had met regular customers who stopped to talk. Most were mill hands in the factory, some worked in the warehouses along Front Street and a few were merchants and businessmen.

Jamie asked a couple of people who were foremen if they knew anyone looking for workers, but both said it was hopeless. "Too much unemployment this year," one commented. "Unless this depression lets up I don't know where a young slip of a lad like you might find work."

By the time he had sold his last paper it was after nine. It was turning into a beautiful day, even warmer than the day before, and Jamie took his time getting back to the *Globe* office. When he got there he had all but forgotten Stinger.

"Over here," the blond boy motioned. He was sitting with Bud and Paddy. Jamie glanced around guiltily, but he crossed the yard to join them. Stinger got to his feet and ordered the boys to follow him. They went out of the yard and walked a block away to the grassed area in front of the Anglican cathedral on Church Street.

Stinger was tense and excited. "I got it all figured out. We's gonna make a fortune." He glanced around, his face flushed. "Now that we've got Darnby lined up and our island hideout, it's just perfect."

"What do you mean?" Paddy was skeptical.

"Tonight we're gonna begin. Just the four of us. We're gonna strike quick and fast. They won't know what hit 'em. I've got it figured out exactly. Just stick with Stinger, here, and we're all gonna be rich."

"What do you want from us?" Paddy asked.

"You're my friends. I want you to be part of this thing."

"But how? What do we have to do?"

Stinger glanced around guiltily again. "We work together and then you've got your hideout. It's just perfect for us. If we stick together then we'll be as safe as sittin' in a church pew."

Bud was shaking his head, a worried look on his face. "I don't know. If the police catch us then we'll be sent away for sure."

"But they ain't gonna get us. No one knows about your hideout. They'll never think to look over on the island."

Jamie looked at each of the boys in turn. Stinger's shoulders were hunched, his face tense. The other two boys studied their hands and watched the street.

"I don't want anything to do with this," Jamie announced, trying to keep calm.

All three boys looked at him in surprise. Then Stinger's eyes narrowed and his lips became thin pale lines. "What do you mean?" he demanded angrily.

"Just that I can't be part of this."

"You're already part of it, kid, and you can't get out of it now."

"What do you mean?"

"You was the one who stole the rolls yesterday. Remember?"

"No, I didn't. You took them, Stinger."

"That's not what that copper saw. You was the one who carried them. You was the one who ran."

"But I didn't mean to do it. You put them into my hands."

"The coppers would really like to get an arrest. They told me that. They begged me to testify against you in court, but I said no 'cause you was a friend of mine. I thought you was one of my gang so I protected you. But if you're gonna cut out of this, then…"

"But I didn't do it!" Jamie almost shouted.

"You were the one with the stuff. If I was to testify the judge would send you away to the reformatory for six months. Maybe more."

"It's not fair."

A hard scowl came across Stinger's face. "What's fair in this life, anyway? Either help in these jobs or you're gonna end up with a visit to the police cells. You get my drift?"

Jamie opened his mouth and then closed it again. He had promised Meg he would stay out of trouble, but if he didn't go along Stinger would carry out his threat and then who knew what would happen?

"We're gonna meet at nine o'clock tonight down at Taylor's Wharf," Stinger was saying. "We'll go out and sell the evening papers so no one will be suspicious, and then we'll meet at the wharf. I've got it all planned out. It's gonna work perfectly. Just wait and see."

CHAPTER 6

THE sun was setting in a red glow as Jamie walked along the harbour front. The heat of the humid summer day began to ease, and with darkness falling, the shadows seemed to rise up and enclose him.

The boy passed long sheds and warehouses with blackened empty windows. Riverboats rode at their moorings like silent, darkened palaces. Somewhere behind him a train hissed and fumed as it pulled out of the station. A night watchman passed with a coal-oil lantern swinging in his hand.

What was he to do? The question repeated itself in his mind. If he didn't keep the rendezvous then Stinger would go to the police, but by going he was becoming even more deeply involved.

He shuffled along the dusty road that ran by the water's edge, past empty wagons, stacks of barrels and big wooden crates. Everything was quiet.

"Hey, Jamie. Over here." Stinger's voice came out of the shadows at the foot of Taylor's Wharf. "Where you been? It's long past nine o'clock."

"I got here as soon as I could."

"Well, you're late. Don't let it happen again."

The boys huddled in the dark shadows of large boxes, whispering quietly.

"Do we really have to do this, Stinger?" Paddy asked plaintively.

"Look. This is gonna make us rich. Understand that? Rich. We ain't got a worry in the world. The whole scheme is gonna work out just perfect."

"But … "

"Do you want to keep living like we do? Livin' in dirty, small rooms. Eatin' crusts of bread. I've had it with bein' poor. Stop worrying. Nobody will ever get us. Me and Darnby's got it all figured out."

The boys drew together, crouching in the shadows of the huge boxes as Stinger explained his plans.

"Now, listen good. Jamie, I want you to stay with the boat and be ready for us. You other two come with me, and let's stick close together. I don't want nothin' messed up."

"Where's the boat?" Jamie asked.

"She's tied up down at the end of the dock," Bud explained.

"You be careful, kid," Stinger said. "Stay out of sight and keep quiet. We don't need nobody gettin' suspicious. You go ahead first."

Slowly Jamie got to his feet and walked towards the wharf. In the west there was still a hint of pale light that was quickly fading into black. Overhead a million stars were beginning to come out. The boy's feet clumping on the boards of the wharf sounded in his ears like half an army. He glanced around anxiously, but there was no one to pay any attention. At the end of the wharf he found the skiff bobbing gently against a big wooden post. As he climbed over the side he looked back and could see the dark shapes of the three boys — one tall and two short — walking towards the city.

Jamie sat in the boat and listened as the water lapped against the sides. Carefully he looked in every direction, expecting to find someone watching, but there was only the dark water and a few lights on the distant shore. Slowly he undid the line holding the bow and eased the boat under the wharf in among the shadows of the cribs and pilings of its foundation. He tied it up again and sat waiting.

It was very quiet. The inky black water rose and sank gently with the easy swells, lapping softly against the hull of the skiff and washing the pilings. In the distance there were sounds of trains occasionally blowing their haunting whistles, and the city gave off a dull hum.

As he was sitting there the sky in the east grew lighter and then a full moon rose out of the low horizon. The large yellowish globe cast an eerie light as it gleamed on the water and danced with the soft ripples on the surface.

Jamie listened intently. Whenever a person walked along the harbour road he concentrated on the sound of the crunch of gravel until he was convinced it was receding. Once he froze in terror as someone came onto the wharf. Big footsteps creaked the timbers. Through the cracks of the boards he could see the yellow light of a lantern. His breathing came hard. Maybe it was the police. But then, as suddenly as they had come, the footsteps disappeared and an uneasy silence returned.

What if the police found him in the boat? What if Stinger and the others had been caught? Why were they taking so long? Maybe he should just leave — go back home to tell Meg everything that had happened. Maybe he should get out before it was too late.

But if he was to desert he was sure that Stinger would go to the police and then it would be jail. And could he leave Bud and Paddy to face all of this alone? Perhaps things would be all right. Maybe Stinger knew what he was doing.

Suddenly there were hurried footsteps on the deck of the wharf. He felt his body tense, and his heart beat loudly.

"Jamie! Jamie, where are you?" It was Stinger's urgent whispered voice.

As fast as he could the boy untied the skiff and manoeuvred it between the pilings to the end of the dock. In the moonlight he saw Stinger carrying a big canvas sack over his shoulder. He was smiling. Paddy was looking back towards the city as if someone was following them, and Bud bent down to hold the boat.

Stinger swung his sack over the side, dropped it into the bow and climbed down after it. Within moments the other two boys had scrambled into the stern and Jamie was rowing with long rapid strokes out into Toronto Bay.

"Everything go all right?" Jamie whispered.

Stinger laughed under his breath. "Easy as eatin' rhubarb pie. I snuck in through the window of this house, quiet as a cat, and it was easy pickin's. The people were probably off at a prayer meetin', while I was inside helpin' myself to all the loot I could carry." And he laughed out loud.

"Where were Bud and Paddy?"

"Lookouts. You got to have lookouts in an outfit like this. We're a smooth team. That's what we are." Again he laughed loud enough to send the sound clear across the harbour.

Jamie rowed them through the ink-black water with the pale moon over his right shoulder. As they went out into the water they could see riverboats tied at their wharves and the tall masts of schooners riding gently at anchor. The dim light from thousands of gas street lamps lit up the city with a warm glow.

Jamie had never seen Stinger in such a good mood. "Come on, boy," he said. "Lean into them oars. We're gonna have a good time tonight."

The other two boys were subdued. Paddy kept dangling his hand in the water and looking back at the city as it receded. Bud's usual carefree smile had been replaced by a sober look.

As they rowed across the bay Stinger kept talking. "Me Dad and I used to fish out in this bay. Used to catch whitefish and perch and trout, and we'd go up on one of them beaches on the island and fry 'em up over a big fire. In the season we'd catch salmon as they ran up the Don River and there'd be ice fishin' in the winter.

"What happened to your father?" Jamie asked.

"Disappeared. One day seven, maybe eight years ago he told me I was old enough to look after myself and he just left. I've been on my own ever since."

"You must miss him."

Stinger thought for a moment. "I got along ... I survived."

"And your mother?"

"Heard she was an Englishwoman, but I never knew her."

"Didn't you ever go to school, Stinger?"

"I learned to write me own name. And I can do 'rithmetic real good. That's enough. I got my wits. If you're gonna survive as a street boy you got to be smart and quick. You got to know every scheme in town, and I know 'em all."

They drifted into silence again. All they could hear was the dip of the oars and the gentle slap of water as the bow sliced through the calm black surface of the bay.

"We're gettin' in close," said Paddy suddenly. "Pull a little on your left hand, Jamie. That's good."

Jamie looked over his shoulder and found they were just a few yards off the beach. The tall willow trees with their long dangling leaves enclosed the shore. A cluster of bulrushes waved gently at the swampy edge.

"There's a fire!" whispered Bud suddenly, a touch of panic in his voice. "At our campsite. See it there?"

Jamie stopped rowing and they drifted. Now he could see the flames of a fire casting a glare up into the leaves of the trees.

"Have the coppers found us already?" Paddy hissed.

Stinger laughed. "Don't be stupid. It's Darnby. I told him to meet us here."

"Are you sure it's him?" Paddy asked uncertainly.

"Of course I'm sure." The big boy stood up in the bow of the boat. "Darnby!" he called. "Is that you?"

A dark form materialized on the narrow beach. "Are you fellas gonna raise the whole neighbourhood?" And they heard his laugh echo across the water.

Stinger's laugh joined his. "We don't have nothin' to worry about. Them coppers are chasin' each other all over the city and here we are sittin' out on the island safe as a bed bug."

"So it was a successful expedition?"

The hull of the boat slid onto the sand bottom. Stinger held up the canvas bag and shook it until it rattled. "It's a beginning."

"Good. That's the way I like to see it work, boys. Come ashore, and let's see what you've got."

They climbed over the side and into the shallow water. Stinger waded ashore with his bag over his shoulder and went with Darnby to sit by the fire while the other three steered the skiff into its mooring behind the fallen tree. There they found Darnby's rowboat.

It was dark back there. The only light came from the glow of the fire. "I don't know about this stealing business," Jamie whispered.

"Do you think we're gonna get caught?" asked Bud. "Maybe we should go to the police before it's too late."

Paddy was shaking his head. "The police would charge us, and then who knows what would happen?"

"But we're just going to get into deeper and deeper trouble."

They could see Darnby and Stinger by the fire, excitedly extracting things from the canvas bag.

"Look at this silver candlestick," they could hear Stinger saying. "We're gonna make a fortune, Darnby. I can feel it. We'll have money comin' in and you and me will go off somewhere and live in a rich man's house, and have nice clothes, and ... maybe a dog ... and everythin'."

"You're goin' to spend it all before you even get it in your hand, Stinger. We've just begun."

"How long before we're rich?"

The fire glowed, making strange shapes and shadows on the trees and on their faces. "This is a gold mine we've fallen into. The island and the boats and Toronto just off there. It's a perfect set up, and we're going to work it till the well runs dry."

As the three boys came into the light of the fire, Darnby and Stinger quickly put the loot back into the bag.

"My four little outlaws," said Darnby. "You all did very well tonight. This here's gonna be a real neat arrangement. We're a well-coordinated team. It's going to be the end of poverty for us all."

"What's your part, Mr. Darnby?" Jamie asked.

"That's a good question, boy. I'm going to be responsible for the merchandise. For the disposal of the property, and it's an important part of the job, if I have to say so myself. It's dangerous ... very dangerous ... with risks so high it makes the actual robberies seem like child's play."

"But who will look after the money?" Bud asked.

"Why, Stinger and me, of course. We hain't gonna give a job of such importance to one of you young people. We have to have a person we can all trust."

"Who says we can trust you?" pressed Paddy.

"Well, I suppose you fellers are just gonna have to trust us. There hain't no other way." Darnby's face looked flushed.

"You got to understand we're real lucky to have someone like Darnby with us," Stinger said quickly. "He's gonna do all the hard parts. All we have to do is watch the money roll in. There's nothin' to worry about."

Silence descended on the little group. Jamie watched the glowing embers of the fire and tried to think clearly. It seemed to him that they had everything to worry about. They were breaking the law. Where would it all end?

Darnby got up and disappeared into the bush with the canvas bag. When he returned he was chuckling to himself. "You boys ever seen juggling?" he said.

"Can you juggle? Like really juggle with balls and everything?" asked Bud, his eyes wide.

"Didn't I say I was in the circus?"

He had taken three apples out of his pocket and in a moment he had them all in the air at the same time, tossing them from hand to hand in one smooth action.

"Wow!" said Paddy. "Are you ever good."

Darnby caught all of the apples and then settled down by the fire. "All right, you boys need to get some sleep."

Stinger sat up straight. "Tomorrow we have to go in and sell our newspapers. If we don't, Detective Moffat is sure to get suspicious."

Suddenly Jamie remembered. "I've got to go home."

"Home? Are you kiddin'?" said Stinger in surprise. "We ain't gonna row you across the bay at this time of night."

"But Meg will be worried. She'll be waiting."

"Do you got to have your big sister to hold your hand?" Stinger said scornfully.

"Paddy, Bud. Could you row me across to the city?" Jamie pleaded.

"No!" Darnby said sharply. "That sister of yours is going to have to get used to the fact that you're a big boy now. You're one of us. The sooner she understands that the better."

"But … " Jamie knew that all the pleading in the world would do no good. He got up and went down to the beach. Across the still water the city glowed a yellowish golden hue. The pale moon was almost directly overhead. It shone out of a cloudless, star-filled sky, bathing the harbour in a cool white light.

Jamie thought of his sister all by herself in their small room, pacing back and forth as she waited for him to return. He wanted to be part of the gang and stay with the boys, but another part of him wanted to get back to Meg.

"Come on, Jamie," whispered Paddy. The two boys had come up on either side of him.

"We've made up a place for you to sleep," said Bud softly.

Jamie felt close to tears. "It's just that Meg … "

Paddy put his arm over his shoulder. "She'll be all right. It's just for tonight. Come to bed now."

"What's going to happen?" Jamie asked plaintively.

But the boys did not answer. They took their friend's arm and led him to the place where he would sleep.

CHAPTER 7

THE next morning as they rowed across the bay and walked up to the *Globe* building on King Street, Jamie felt sick with worry. The thought that he should go directly home to find his sister went through his mind, but instead he went with the others to the newspaper office. It was there that he found Meg waiting for him. She looked terrible, her eyes etched with red from lack of sleep.

Meg rushed over to them. "Where have you been, Jamie? I waited up all night. I thought maybe the police or … or I didn't know what." She seemed close to tears.

"I was all right."

"But you can't stay out all night."

"Why not? What's wrong with that?" Jamie glanced at the other boys, embarrassed. "Bud and Paddy do it all the time, and they're younger than me."

"Jamie, you're going to get in trouble if you do that. Where were you, anyway?"

"I was with the boys."

"But where did you go?"

Jamie glanced at the others uncomfortably. "It was hot last night, so … " He stumbled for an explanation. "So after we finished selling our papers we went over to the island for a swim."

"But why didn't you come and tell me?"

"I was going to come home, Meg. It was going to be just a quick dip and the boys were going to bring me back, but we got playing around and it got too late. We decided to stay at their camp for the rest of the night." Jamie looked at the others uneasily. The lying came too naturally.

Meg turned away from her brother. When she turned back she was calmer. "Jamie, you've got to quit selling newspapers and get a full-time job."

"Why don't you leave the kid alone?" said Stinger, breaking in aggressively.

"But he's my brother. I have to look after him."

"He's a free person. Let him do what he wants."

"Do what he wants? He's only twelve years old."

"That's old enough. I was on my own when I was nine."

"And look at you, Stinger." Meg was annoyed now. "If you think I want my brother to end up like you, then think again."

"I don't care what nobody thinks of me," Stinger laughed contemptuously. "Jamie's one of us now. He's gonna live like a street boy. Live by his wits and be free."

Meg took her brother's arm and steered him over to the window. The other boys went to join the end of the line, but Stinger continued to stare at Meg with a surly snarl on his face.

"Jamie, you've got to listen," Meg whispered. "Doing things like this will get you in trouble. What would Mother say if she knew you were out all night with boys the likes of Stinger?"

"But Stinger's my ... friend. You can't say those things about him." Jamie wasn't sure what to do. He wanted to stay with the boys.

"Friend? Stinger's not a friend of anyone. He's only interested in himself." Meg looked tired and worried. "Jamie, come with me this morning. Maybe you can find work in one of the warehouses."

"There is no work. I've asked and if I don't go out selling my papers then someone will take over my corner. Anyway, I like selling papers. I can be with my friends and have no boss. I'll be good, Meg. Don't worry. I won't get into trouble. But I can't stop selling papers before I get some other work. We need the money. You said so yourself."

Slowly she nodded. There was something terribly wrong, she knew that, but what could she do? "All right," she said, sighing. "But don't stay out all night again. Please!"

Jamie smiled. "I won't, Meg. I promise."

"I've got to go to work now. Come home after you sell the evening papers. We'll do something nice together."

She looked at him with big eyes that seemed to say she knew her worries were far from over. Then she slipped out.

As he watched her go, Jamie felt a pang of guilt. He had lied to his sister, and he felt badly about that, but he didn't want her telling him what to do all the time. He wanted to be free. That was the point. Free to do just what he wanted.

Stinger was still annoyed when Jamie joined them in line. "Who does she think she is, tellin' you what to do like you was a little kid?"

"She's not gonna treat me like that anymore," Jamie said defiantly.

"Good," said Stinger, "'cause we've got a job tonight and we need everyone to do it."

Suddenly Jamie felt panic. "I ... I can't go, Stinger. I promised Meg I'd be home right after I sell the evening papers."

"What are you talkin' about, kid? You just told me you weren't gonna listen to that sister of yours."

It was all a confusion to Jamie. He wanted to be free of Meg's control, he wanted to be accepted by the gang, but ...

"I promised her," he pleaded lamely.

Now the pressmen were dumping big stacks of newspapers on the counter. The boys and girls began to move forward.

Stinger grabbed Jamie's arm and squeezed hard. "You're gonna do what I tell you, kid, and I say we've got a job to do tonight."

"But I told you I can't!"

The line was moving. Stinger pulled Jamie's arm and swung him around so that their faces were only inches apart. "You'll do as I say or them coppers will find you in three pieces, kid." The veins of his neck stood out. His teeth gritted together as he spat out the words.

"You're hurting my arm, Stinger."

"It'll hurt a lot more if you don't do what I say. We've got a job tonight and you're going to be there."

Jamie quickly paid for one hundred papers and escaped without saying anything more. As he got to the door he heard Stinger calling for him to stop, but he ignored him. When he got to the street he ran west two blocks as far as Bay before he felt safe enough to slow to a walk.

Already it was a hot, humid day. The sun beat down out of a pale blue haze. The dust of the streets rose every time a horse and wagon passed. Fancy women were out in sun bonnets and carrying parasols, and some businessmen had slipped off their jackets.

When Jamie got to his corner at Bay and Front streets he began to sell his papers and tried to forget about his problems.

"*Globe*! Get your *Globe* here. Crime wave continues. Ned Hanlan, Toronto's world famous sculler, wins another race. Get your *Globe* here." As he chanted the customers flocked to him.

Close to the seven a.m. starting time of the furniture factory there was a rush of customers. The boy dealt out papers and took change as fast as he could. But the last twenty papers took two hours to sell, and by the time he was finished he felt dead on his feet.

It was after nine when he got back to the *Globe*. He looked for the other boys but couldn't find them so he stretched out on the soft grass and listened to the chatter of some of the other sellers. He was tired from the late night and the restless sleep on the hard ground. Soon he drifted off.

"Jamie, wake up." He felt a sharp nudge in his rib cage. Towering over him was Stinger who was poking him with his foot. "You and me's gonna settle things once and for all."

Jamie looked around for Paddy and Bud but they were nowhere to be seen. Stinger motioned for him to follow and walked across the yard to the street. The big sixteen-year-old led the way to the church the next block over and sat down on the grass. Jamie perched a little ways from him.

"You're comin' tonight, kid. I got it all planned out. We're gonna make a fortune and tonight's a big night."

"I don't know, Stinger."

"You're gonna do it." Stinger leaned over to whisper the words for emphasis. "You know too much to pull out now. You could squeal to them coppers. Either you're one of us or you're an enemy. Join us or I'm gonna come huntin' for you."

Jamie felt himself cringe. "What do you mean?"

"Just let me say it ain't gonna be pleasant. I've got lots of nasty things that I can do to you. That's one thing I know a lot about."

Stinger got to his feet. In Jamie's eyes he looked huge. "You be down at the dock by nine tonight, kid. If you're not there, then watch out 'cause I'm gonna be comin' to look for you." He left, walking hurriedly along King Street.

Slowly Jamie got up and started walking back to the *Globe* building. He shuffled along, staring at the ground. Stinger was going to force him into a life of crime and then what would happen?

Still Bud and Paddy were not back at the *Globe*. He wanted to talk to them so badly. He felt they were the only ones who would understand. Even Meg was like a stranger to him now. If only he could talk to the boys maybe they could find a way out of this mess together, but they were nowhere to be found.

That morning he walked slowly along the harbour front looking at the boats and watching the stevedores work. A riverboat came into the Yonge Street dock from Niagara-on-the-Lake. He watched the passengers crowd off and for a time listened to a fiddler playing for pennies.

At about noon he went and got the shoe shine kit and worked in front of the Queen's Hotel for awhile. Afterwards he ate some fruit he bought from a street seller and wandered up to have a big bowl of ice cream at the Italian confectionery store. At four he collected seventy copies of the *Mail*, one of the evening papers. He was hoping to see Paddy and Bud getting papers themselves, but they didn't turn up. What could have happened to them? Had they pulled out of the operation?

It was eight-thirty by the time he had hawked his last paper. Still he hadn't decided what to do. Meg would be waiting for him at home and Stinger was down at the docks.

Slowly he walked down by the waterfront, along the Esplanade heading east. The scorching, humid heat of the day was lifting and the sun was a red ball in the west, spreading gold on light fluffy clouds high in the sky. Through the dying light he could see across to

Taylor's Wharf. There, sitting on a cluster of barrels, were three boys: two small and one almost the size of a man.

Jamie stood on the corner for a long time and then, deliberately, went to join them. He wanted to be with the others. He wanted to be one of the gang.

"Jamie, good to see you." Bud and Paddy both had smiles of welcome. Even Stinger seemed pleased.

"Where have you two been all day?" Jamie asked.

"We went to the island for a rest. Felt tired after last night."

"All right, quit talkin'," Stinger ordered. "We've got plans to make."

Night was coming. As they talked it grew dim and the sky turned black.

Up on the Esplanade the lamplighter was going his rounds, turning on each of the gas lamps one at a time. Candles were lit in windows and people walked with lanterns swinging in their hands. There was a hush on the city.

The plan was different that night. Stinger had spotted a warehouse he wanted to break into, but it was going to be tricky to get the stuff out of the building and down to the dock without being seen. He had found a rickety hand cart somewhere and it was Jamie's job to look after it. As the boy pushed it up the incline the wooden wheels wobbled and made a crunching sound on the roadway that seemed loud enough to attract everyone within a mile.

They went over the railway tracks and up Sherbourne Street, following the darkest path possible. On the corner of Front Street was a tavern with a bright gas lamp illuminating the area. They could hear loud laughter and the voices of longshoremen and sailors.

"It's down here," Stinger whispered.

Jamie steered the cart down a narrow cobblestone alley, the wheels scraping and bumping over every stone. It was very dark. On each side of them were stone and brick walls rising two and three storeys.

"Here it is. This here window's open. I checked it this afternoon." Stinger pushed it up as quietly as possible. "All right, you two get inside," he ordered Bud and Paddy. "And Jamie, hide the cart over in the shadows there. Be ready to take the furs when we pass them out. If you see coppers give the whistle like I showed you."

The two smaller boys slipped inside and Stinger followed. Jamie parked the cart and stood in the darkness, waiting and watching.

He could feel his heart thumping in his chest. Up and down the alleyway he looked, back and forth. On Sherbourne he heard the noise of loud voices. Three men went past, heading towards the harbour. Slowly their sounds faded away. A little later a horse and wagon went trotting by and then two more people.

Inside the warehouse Jamie caught glimpses of the boys. They had lit matches to help them search the darkness. When the light flickered out they would light another. What could be taking them so long?

He had been watching the Sherbourne Street entrance to the alleyway because that was where most of the activity was coming from, and did not see the policeman at first. Then he heard a fresh noise. He glanced around quickly and saw a man wearing the distinctive helmet coming towards him.

For an instant Jamie couldn't move. He couldn't give the signal. He just plastered himself against the brick wall, wishing he could melt into it. Then he whistled three notes, low and long.

"What are you doing here, boy?" the policeman demanded sharply.

Jamie saw the matches go out and thought he heard a quick scurrying of feet.

"I heard that whistle! What was it all about?" The officer came up with long strides.

Inside the warehouse there was not a sound now. Not a hint of movement.

Jamie swallowed hard. "It was nothing, sir. I was just whistling a tune."

The policeman examined him carefully. He was a broad-shouldered man with a handlebar moustache. "What are you doing in a back alley like this late at night?"

Sweat poured from the boy. "Just getting some air, sir. It was hot in my room."

Jamie was sure he caught sight of Stinger's pale face in the window over the policeman's shoulder, but then it was gone.

"My room is sweltering. This weather's awful." Slowly he began walking towards Sherbourne Street, leaving the cart behind. "Aren't you hot wearing that big heavy helmet and jacket?"

"It's pretty warm."

"Why do they make you wear such heavy things in summer?"

"Regulations. The police chief thinks we have to look formal even if we die of the heat."

They had reached Sherbourne Street now. The noise from the tavern was even louder and the policeman made his way up towards the corner. "You get on home now, boy. Don't be loitering on the streets."

"Yes, sir. Good night."

Jamie thought about doubling back to meet the others, but he knew it was too dangerous. They would have to get out of the warehouse and fend for themselves. He was going home to see Meg.

CHAPTER 8

R ASH of Robberies Continues," blared out the morning's headlines of the *Globe*.

Jamie had picked up a discarded paper as he was coming into the building and read the article as he stood in line waiting for his papers. It reported that altogether there had been five break-ins or suspected break-ins the previous evening, and went on to give a detailed account of a suspected robbery of a fur warehouse that had been discovered by a police officer around midnight. But it was the next paragraph that gave the boy a real chill.

"Police suspect some of the robberies have been carried out by children. Earlier last evening young boys were seen loitering around the fur warehouse and only later was it discovered that an attempt had been made to enter the premises. Police have concluded that these boys were involved in this break-in."

The article finished with a quote from the police chief. "Delinquent boys are becoming a serious problem in Toronto. Many have no families, they live on the street with no means of support, and they engage in petty thievery. Something must be done to control them or this crime wave will get even worse."

Jamie closed the newspaper. He looked around at the room crowded with boys and girls waiting for their papers and wondered uneasily if anyone suspected that he was involved in this sorry mess. He was relieved to see Bud, Paddy and Stinger come into the room a few moments later.

Stinger seemed angry. He motioned to Jamie and the four of them huddled by the window. "What happened to you last night?" he asked sharply.

"The policeman showed up and I gave the signal," Jamie said defensively.

"But then you left."

"I had to get him away from the warehouse so you could get out. If I had circled around to meet you and he had spotted me, he would have been even more suspicious."

Stinger's eyes narrowed. "Maybe you arranged to have the coppers show up to catch us."

Jamie glanced at the others, but they were all looking at him skeptically. "Look, if I wanted you to get caught there would have been a dozen policemen waiting for you when you came out of the warehouse."

Paddy nodded. "Jamie's right. He did the smart thing."

"All right, but I don't trust you much, kid. Remember that. As far as I'm concerned you still have to prove yourself and I'm going to be watching you all the time."

They were about to rejoin the line when Jamie called them back. "Hey, did you see the article in the paper about us?" he whispered.

"What article?" Bud asked.

Jamie opened his newspaper. "Look at that headline. They know all about us."

The boys crowded around, looking over Jamie's shoulder. Paddy was mouthing the words, but Stinger and Bud had blank stares on their faces.

"What's it say?" asked the older boy.

"Can't you read it?"

"Just tell me what it says."

Jamie started with the headlines and went on to read the column. When he got to the part about the attempted break-in of the fur warehouse, Stinger was smiling.

"Listen to that. We got 'em on the run," he said with satisfaction.

"It means they're closing in on us. That's what it means."

"They're not going to get anyone. Read some more."

Stinger loved the part about the police chief. He laughed right out loud. "That old fool couldn't tell a robber from a rabbit."

"I'll tell the chief that is your opinion of him, Stinger." It was Detective Moffat, tall and lean and serious. How long had he been listening? Beside him was the blond uniformed policeman who had been with him the night he had visited Jamie.

Jamie dropped the paper. Paddy and Bud looked horrified, but Stinger just laughed again.

"Tell us what you know about those break-ins," Moffat said calmly.

"We don't tell coppers nothin'. You're the police around here. You can find out what's goin' on yourself."

"Maybe I think it's you, Stinger, and this gang of street urchins that you lead, that are doing all of the break-ins."

The boy laughed. "If it was us then I can tell you, Moffat, that you ain't never going to catch us."

"Is that a fact? Do you think we're stupid, Stinger?"

"Yeah, that's right. I think you're stupid. I think you're so stupid you couldn't catch a crook with his hand in the cookie jar. That's how stupid I think you are." He was standing with both hands on his hips.

"Well, just watch out. The next time you put your hand in the cookie jar there might be something inside waiting to sting you."

Stinger laughed again. "I do the stingin' around here. That's how I got my name."

"Don't be so sure, boy."

Moffat drifted away, and the four boys went to join the end of the line. Jamie watched the detective closely. He stopped to talk to several newspaper sellers, said a few words and then moved on. Quietly the boy crept close enough to hear. He was talking to a young girl.

"Know any boys flashing a lot of money, Annabel?"

The girl looked at him out of big innocent eyes. "Oh, no, sir. Everybody's poor around here."

"Heard of anyone involved in these break-ins?"

"No, sir. No one."

The policeman moved on and began to question someone else. But if they knew who was doing the robberies, no one in that room was going to tell the police. A few minutes after he had come in Moffat and his partner made for the door. He paused for a moment, staring at Stinger, and then left.

"Look at him go. Just like a snake slitherin' away in the grass. He ain't never gonna find nothin'."

"I don't like it," Jamie was whispering. "Stories about the break-ins are in the newspapers. Detective Moffat's coming around. Things are getting too hot for us."

"Don't be crazy. You don't know how stupid these coppers are. I've been runnin' circles around 'em for years."

"But we've been caught before, too," said Paddy. "If any of us go up before the judge again ... "

"You don't have to worry. You're with Stinger now. This is the big time. You'll never get caught with me."

"But it almost happened last night," said Bud.

"Just an accident. A freak. It happens sometimes."

Jamie was shaking his head. "But the police are looking for us. Our luck is bound to run out."

"Never, kid, never. I tell you we're gonna make a fortune."

Jamie looked to the others. "What do you think, Paddy?"

"Maybe Jamie's right."

Now Stinger turned angry. "Never!" he whispered angrily between his teeth. "We got a job tonight and we're gonna do it. I've scouted this place, and we got to do it tonight. We'll meet down at the wharf at nine, and you'd all better be there."

After their morning sales Jamie met Bud and Paddy back at the *Globe* building and they spent a lazy day together. First they wandered down to the harbour, walked west as far as the old garrison and then hiked up the railway line to the glass and steel Crystal Palace. The three boys sprawled out on the lawn and took off their shirts to let the sweating hot sun bake them. Soon they were again talking about the mess they were in.

"You should see that Darnby guy," said Bud, brightening for a moment. "Is he ever a good acrobat. Yesterday he was out at our camp showin' how he could do cartwheels and stand on his hands and all that stuff."

"Is he out there all the time?" asked Jamie.

"Well, lots of times."

For a long time the boys lay on their backs feeling the hot sun and sweating in the humid air. High clouds were forming out over the lake and shifted about in different directions.

Finally Jamie sat up on one elbow. "Maybe we shouldn't go tonight. Maybe we should tell him we're not going to be a part of his gang anymore."

Paddy shook his head. "Can't do that. Stinger would come and get us in our camp, or he might go to Moffat and blame us for all the break-ins. He'd get revenge. He's like that."

"But we're running a big risk if we go on."

"Is it any worse than having someone like Stinger after us?"

There seemed to be nothing more to be said. They were frightened. Even Jamie had to accept the fact that there was nothing he could do but go along.

Later the boys walked through the grounds of the mental asylum, a large domed building with tall pillars at the front entrance. When they got to Queen Street they headed east to the city centre.

In the evening the weather began to change. Jamie was selling papers when he noticed the sky suddenly darken. From the west, dark turbulent clouds were rolling into the city. A gentle far-off rumble of thunder announced a storm. By eight-thirty, when he had sold his last paper, the sky was blackening, the wind was picking up scraps of paper. People were beginning to scurry for shelter.

Jamie cut down to the waterfront and began heading east along the roadway that ran in front of the wharves. Behind him there was a flash of lightning. He turned around. A gigantic black cloud was overhead, rumbling and churning, spitting out shafts of lightning in jagged flashes. Longshoremen were covering wagonloads of goods with tarpaulins. Teamsters were fleeing with their horses. Seamen battened down hatches and stripped the remaining sails from their vessels. The boy hurried.

Suddenly big drops of rain smacked into the dusty road and chopped the surface of the water of the harbour. Jamie broke into a run. Overhead the sky boiled. The rain was washing into his hair and soaking his shirt but he ran on, almost blinded by the downpour.

"Jamie! Jamie! Over here!"

There in among big discarded wooden boxes he saw the huddled forms of Bud, Paddy and Stinger, trying to stay dry in a makeshift shelter.

"Come on!" shouted Bud above the noise of the storm. "There's room."

Jamie crawled in beside Bud. With the rain hammering down on the wooden roof it was too noisy to talk, but the closeness made it cozy, and it was almost dry.

Across the railway tracks on the Esplanade people were huddled in doorways waiting for the downpour to pass. A hansom cab splashed along, its fine black Arabian horse skittish and frightened. Big dirty puddles grew in the roadway.

Darkness came quickly. Somewhere behind the black clouds the sun went down. The rainfall intensified. Thunder rolled above them. Soon the buildings on the other side of the railway tracks disappeared from view and all they could make out was the dim glow of the gas lamps along the Esplanade.

"We should go home," Jamie said, but his words disappeared into the storm. He turned and spoke loudly enough for the others to hear. "The weather's too miserable. We should go home and forget about this job tonight."

"Weather's perfect," Stinger answered loudly. "Just right."

"But the rain … "

"Coppers won't be out on a night like this."

"But … "

"Quiet!" Stinger ordered. "We're doin' the job and no arguments."

Jamie peered out into the rainstorm. What could he say? Nothing would deter Stinger now. Then, gradually, the storm eased. The cloud moved off to the east, taking with it the rumbling and flashes of lightning.

Stinger gathered his legs under him. "All right, let's get ready. We're going to move."

Paddy protested. "It hasn't stopped raining."

"It will give us more cover." He paused for a moment. "Jamie, stay with the boat. See it's bailed out and ready to go. You other two stay close behind me. This might be tricky, but it won't take long. Let's go."

They left on a run with Stinger in the lead and the other two close behind. In a moment they were swallowed up in the blackness.

Jamie sat in the shelter for a moment longer listening to the storm in the distance. It was colder now. He huddled into his light cotton shirt and then began to move to keep warm.

Quickly he hurried to the end of the wharf, walking carefully so he would not slip on the slick boards. At the end of the dock rode the skiff, half filled with water. He climbed down to it and, standing on a seat to keep his feet dry, he untied the boat and manoeuvred it under the wharf to get some protection from the rain. Then he bailed it out as fast as he could.

It was still raining and the water dripped through the boards above his head. He looked out at the rain chopping the surface of the water, and felt the rhythm of the waves. All the time he thought of his friends. Where were they? Stinger had said it wouldn't take long but still they weren't back.

He wondered about Meg waiting for him in their room on King Street. What would she think if she knew what he was up to?

What could be taking them so long? Where were they? The minutes stretched out until Jamie lost track of how long they had been away.

The rain seemed to be coming down more heavily again. In the west there were more flashes of lightning and rumbles of thunder. Another storm was sweeping in. The winds were picking up, the swells were rising and falling, slapping into the cribs and pilons around him. Rain was turning the surface of the harbour into a foam.

"Jamie!" He thought he heard his name being called. The storm stifled sounds like a blanket. "Jamie!" It came again, louder and more distinct. Then he heard the noise of running feet. "Jamie, get the boat out! Hurry!" It was Stinger.

Quickly Jamie untied the bow rope and brought the boat to the end of the dock. Stinger was standing in the downpour panting hard. A heavy canvas bag was over his shoulder. He stepped into the stern.

"Go! Paddle!" he shouted above the storm.

"Where are the others?"

"The police! Coppers! They got 'em. Let's get out of here!"

Jamie was thunderstruck. "Police! Were they caught?"

"Row, kid! Row, or it's going to happen to us!"

In a panic Jamie pulled away from the shore, rowing with all the strength in his back and arms. They were no more than a few yards off shore when he heard more running feet.

"Stinger! Jamie! Come back!"

Jamie was paralyzed. "It's Bud! He's on the wharf!" He started to turn the boat around.

"Don't go back," Stinger shouted.

"They'll get caught! We have to pick them up!"

"Keep rowing, I tell you!"

"Jamie! Stinger! Come back! Please come back!" Now it was Paddy.

"We've got to help them." Jamie's tears washed his already wet face.

"If you turn this boat I'll split your head open!"

Just then they could make out two, then three policemen coming onto the dock. There was a brief struggle, and Bud and Paddy were captured.

"Row, kid! Row!" Stinger ordered.

"Stop! This is the police! You two in the boat! Come back! I order you!"

But Jamie rowed as hard as he could until the figures at the end of the wharf disappeared into the rainstorm.

CHAPTER 9

"WHY didn't we go back for them when we had the chance?" Jamie raged into the storm, the rain washing his face. It was more than anger he felt. He had betrayed his best friends. "We should have waited for them, Stinger!"

"Row, kid! Row and keep quiet!"

And row he did. The swelling waves heaved the little skiff onto crests and then dropped it into deep troughs. He rowed to keep the bow into the waves so they would not get swamped, and he rowed to escape the police. The rain poured down, soaking them to the skin and chopping the water into foam.

"You deserted them, Stinger! You left them to the police!"

"The coppers were chasing us!"

"You only worried about yourself!" Jamie shouted at the dark form huddled in the stern of the boat. "We could have waited for them!"

"The coppers would have got us all if we waited."

"You were only interested in saving your own skin. I hate you!"

A howling wind was driving the rain before it. Waves broke into whitecaps as they crested and foamed on either side of the small boat. As each wave swept under them they wallowed into the next trough and then climbed unsteadily up to the next crest.

"Pull on the oars or we'll capsize!"

Jamie rowed with all the strength in his arms and back. Suddenly the wind caught the bow and blew them off course. Before he could correct it the next wave caught them sideways and as they fell into the trough it seemed like they were going to roll over. But with a powerful sweep of an oar the boy brought the bow into the waves again. He knew there was no time to argue now. He was rowing for their lives.

The darkness was complete. There was not a sign of life, not a light anywhere. The rain pelted down, making an impenetrable curtain. The black clouds rumbled and thundered, giving sudden flashes of lightning that streaked across the sky. Those fractions of a second revealed a ghostly scene of Toronto Harbour awash in a raging torrent, and showed Stinger, sitting immobile in the stern, holding his canvas bag up against his chest, his eyes wide, his mouth open, mesmerized with fear.

It was up to Jamie to pull them through. His arms were aching, his back shooting with pain, but still he rowed with all the strength in his body. The storm worsened. Now the waves were cresting all around him. The wind was a deafening howl.

With each flash of lightning Jamie tried to look around. They had pulled a long way away from the complex of wharves now but seemed to be no closer to the island. He was rowing with his back to the bow of the boat, and he tried to see where they were going, but the flashes of lightning died before he could turn around.

Water was sloshing into the bottom of the boat. As they crested a high wave a foaming whitecap came dangerously close to the gunwales.

"Stinger! You've got to start bailing," he shouted. But the boy remained a darkened, hunched-up form, clutching his bag in terror.

Jamie shouted again. "You've got to bail, Stinger! We're taking on water!" But still he didn't move.

The boy was at the point of exhaustion now. His arms and back ached from the effort, and his hands were sore from gripping the oars.

Gusts of wind drove the rain at them like stinging pellets. The bay was a heaving turmoil of boiling waves. Overhead the black sky rumbled and churned, spitting out bolts of lightning like they were being delivered from the white-hot furnace of a god. The thunder that followed cracked as if the world was splitting from end to end.

"Stinger! You've got to bail! Bail, Stinger, or we're done for."

"I can't do it, Jamie! I can't!" A flash of lightning showed his face wet with rain and ghostly pale.

The boat was wallowing deeper now. A wave lapped over the bow. "You've got to bail, Stinger! We could go under!"

With Jamie's words lashing him, Stinger began. With one hand still clutching the canvas bag he used the other to dip the pail into the water sloshing around in the bottom of the boat and flung it into the night.

Suddenly there was a prolonged flash of lightning. Jamie managed to turn around and found that they had wandered off course and were heading towards the eastern entrance of the harbour. That was the reason the waves were so high. They were sweeping in from the open water of Lake Ontario. He would have to head farther west, but to do that the boat would have to run a course diagonally across the waves. It was dangerous, but he had to take the risk.

Carefully he swung the bow of the skiff westward. The next wave lapped up the side, and then the boat skidded dangerously at an angle down into the trough. He had turned too far and had to strain to bring the bow back into the waves.

Jamie rowed and rowed, concentrating on the motion of the boat until he knew instinctively what was happening. He rowed with the lash of the rain and the wind at his back until suddenly the waves seemed to ease.

At first he didn't believe what had happened. He dipped the oars twice more and found they were drifting in water as calm as a pond. The rain continued, the wind surged around them in gusts, but the waves had died. With the next flash of lightning Jamie saw that they had moved into the lee of the island and were only a few yards off shore. Finally he could slump on the oars and rest.

"You ain't gonna leave us here, are you?" asked Stinger sharply.

Jamie looked at the darkened form no more than three feet away from him. Now he felt no fear of the big boy. "I've got a mind to dump you overboard for all you've done, Stinger."

"Don't be smart, kid. Come on. Let's get back to camp."

The boy was too exhausted to answer. He rested for a moment longer and then slowly began to row again. They searched the shore for the camp. It took a long time but finally they spotted a familiar weeping willow tree hanging over the water and brought the skiff onto the beach.

"Stinger, is that you?" Darnby's voice came from shore.

"Yes. We're here."

Now they could see him standing on the narrow beach. "The night's like a message from the gods. I was flooded out. But how did you fare?"

The bow of the boat scraped bottom. Stinger climbed over the side holding up the canvas bag. "We've got the whole business here, Darnby. It's all in this bag."

"Did you get everything?" There was an excited laugh.

"Yeah, everything worth taking."

"Didn't I say it would be worth it going back to the warehouse?"

Stinger waded ashore and climbed the bank. Then he turned and said to Jamie, "Put the boat away, kid. Darnby and me's got business to talk about."

Jamie let the boat drift. He was drained of all his strength. His arms ached and his back felt like every muscle had been strained to the point of torture.

Darnby hadn't even noticed that Paddy and Bud were not with them, and Stinger hadn't thought to mention it. That was all they felt about those boys. Their only concern was with what was in the bag and how much money they would make.

Somehow Darnby had managed to keep a fire going in spite of the downpour. They built up the flames and Jamie could see the two of them in the glow opening Stinger's sack and going through it eagerly.

Slowly he climbed out of the boat and began easing it into its mooring behind the tree, beside Darnby's skiff. Already his muscles were stiffening. Now that the tension was gone he felt exhausted. All he wanted to do was lie down somewhere and sleep until morning. But as he climbed up the bank and saw the two huddled around the fire, his anger returned.

They were gloating over the loot. In the dim light of the fire he could not see what was in the bag, but he could hear what was being said.

"You really did it this time, Stinger. She's like winnin' a big stakes horse race."

"Think we'll end up with a lot of mo..."

"No tellin' how much she'll bring... big-gest haul I've ever seen." Darnby... out of his pocket, took a swig and passed i... ...ger.

"We're gonna be rich." The boy was excited. "I can feel it. I always felt I'd be rich and have a big house and dogs and everythin'."

Jamie got to his feet. He felt nothing but contempt for the two of them. As he began to move around Darnby glanced up at him suspiciously. Quickly he stuffed the loot back into the bag and then disappeared into the underbrush towards a big willow tree. A moment later he returned empty handed.

Jamie looked through the canvas shelter that Paddy and Bud had built for themselves and found some dry clothes. He took off his own things, hung them over branches and dressed warmly. Then he went to stand on the narrow strip of beach to get as far away from the others as possible.

The trees were still dripping, but it had stopped raining. The dark storm clouds had moved off to the east, but he could hear them rumbling faintly in the distance. In the west the sky was starting to clear.

Across the bay the city lay dormant and asleep. A few weak lights gleamed along the harbour front. The brightest was a side-wheeler all lit up as it hosted a glorious ball or banquet for the wealthy.

As he stood watching the scene he gloomily thought of Paddy and Bud. They were the only real friends he'd ever had. What was happening to them now? Marched off to the police station and then …. It seemed too terrible to think about.

If only he had insisted on waiting just a little longer they would have got to the boat. Maybe he should have ignored Stinger, turned the boat around and tried to pick them up at the wharf. But would there have been time? He didn't know. All he could do was torment himself with the possibility that things might have turned out differently if he had tried.

A shudder went through him as he stood on that strip of beach watching the lights of the city. Meg would be waiting for him. He had promised he would return early that night and once again he was going back on his word.

It was his fault. The whole sorry mess was his fault. He understood that now. When it started he should have told Stinger that he wasn't going to get involved in robberies and break-ins, and he should have tried to persuade Paddy and Bud not to get involved, either. But instead he had done nothing. He had allowed himself to be swept along with events because he couldn't say no. Now he was in such deep trouble he feared he would never get out.

Across the water the lights of the city were going out one by one. The clouds were rapidly clearing and even as he stood there the moon, still nearly full, bathed the scene in its pale silver light.

Jamie was calm. Now he knew what he had to do. Early in the morning he would row across to the city, find his sister and tell her everything that had happened. Meg would help him do what was right.

With that resolution he found a tarpaulin and blanket, stretched out on a soft piece of ground near the beach and went to sleep, leaving Stinger and Darnby talking around the fire.

By the 1870s Toronto was a rapidly growing centre of about 75,000 people. The harbour was a busy place with schooners, square riggers and steamers jamming the wharfs. Railroad tracks hugged the waterfront, and the city grew north, stretching across the gently inclining plain.

In summer the waterfront was crowded with every kind of vessel. This steamer, the *City of Toronto*, had a regular run to Niagara.

Sidewheelers carrying passengers and cargo made voyages all through the Great Lakes and down the St. Lawrence to Montreal. This photograph shows the *Picton* and *Chicora* at the Yonge Street wharf.

This drawing shows the paddle steamer *Algerian* taking on passengers at the Yonge Street wharf.

By the 1870s Ontario was crisscrossed with railways that connected Toronto to Montreal in the east, and Hamilton, London, Sarnia and Windsor in the west. There were connections to the north and to major U.S. cities like New York and Chicago. This wood-burning locomotive, *Lady Elgin*, was one of the first used in the province.

Toronto's railway terminal, Union Station, built in 1873, was one of the biggest buildings in the city. Trains could go completely inside to load and unload passengers.

The Queen's Hotel, shown here, was one of the finest establishments in the country. The horse-drawn car in front ran on steel rails. This was one of the city's earliest means of mass transit.

King Street was the centre of the city's commercial district in the 1870s. This is King Street East between Church and Jarvis streets in 1872.

Wooden walkways, like the one in the left foreground, kept Toron-
tonians out of the mud of the street. At night, pedestrians made their
way by the eerie yellow light of gas lanterns. This is King Street
sometime between 1872 and 1876.

St. Lawrence Hall, opened in 1851 on the corner of King and Jarvis streets, was a symbol of the city's growing prosperity.

St. Lawrence Market, across the street from the hall, housed butcher shops and grocery stores. This photo was taken in 1888.

Toronto was a trading centre, but by the 1870s it was also a growing industrial city. The Gooderham and Worts distillery, near the
mouth of the Don River in the east end, was one of the city's largest
employers.

Other industries included steel rolling mills, like the Toronto Rolling Mills, shown here, and furniture factories.

Newspaper publishing became a very important business. This building was home to the *Globe*, which had the highest circulation and the greatest influence. Its publisher, George Brown, was one of the leading political figures of the era.

Papers were sold on the street by news vendors. It was said that a person could hardly walk a block without being approached by "street urchins" trying to make a sale. Many of these children lived on their own and supported themselves entirely by selling newspapers. This drawing is from *The Canadian Illustrated News.*

This constable and detective were part of the growing police force that was developed to deal with poverty and crime.

The city's reformers established institutions such as orphanages and the House of Industry. This picture shows "The Boys' Home" on George Street, erected in 1863 to provide for vagrant or abandoned children and direct them to "honest industry."

Offenders were jailed for the most minor infractions. This jail at
Berkeley and Parliament streets was an imposing, grim structure
overlooking the east end of the harbour.

Prisoners were locked in their cells for long hours, and flogging was a common means of discipline.

Beyond the built-up areas of Toronto were ravines and farm lands. The Don River, shown in this painting, meandered through beautiful pastures and forest. It was a favourite spot for children, who escaped the city heat with a plunge in the Don's cool, clear waters.

One of the most popular recreation areas was the harbour, with the island lying just offshore. Hotels and other recreational facilities on the island catered to people escaping the city. This is Hanlan's Hotel, run by the family of the world-famous rower Ned Hanlan.

Boating, fishing and wandering on the beach were favourite activities for all classes of people. This drawing shows Hanlan's Point on the island.

In the 1870s parts of the island were developed for summer homes, but some of it remained deserted. People from the city could still row or sail across to picnic on a sand bar or camp in a secret place.

CHAPTER 10

IT was dawn. A clean yellow sun rose in the east and began burning off the white mist that steamed from the glassy surface of Toronto Bay. It was ghostly quiet. Water lapped softly against the shore. The willow trees and bulrushes were motionless. Then, somewhere, the high-pitched sound of the cicada announced that it would be another hot summer day.

Jamie stirred and opened his eyes. Quickly he went down to the beach to splash water on his face. For a moment he crouched on his haunches, watching the steam rise, thinking of everything that had happened.

It all came back to him. Bud and Paddy shouting for help from the end of the wharf, Stinger and Darnby examining their loot without a thought to the boys' capture, and his own role in the whole affair.

Now he acted with purpose. Quickly he changed back into his own clothes and folded up the bedding he had used. The others were up now. Darnby was crouching by the fire trying to stir the ashes into life, and Stinger stretched as if he had had a good night's sleep.

Jamie ignored them and went down to the place where they kept the boats. He began bailing out Paddy and Bud's skiff with a pail they kept in the stern. All the time only one thought went through his mind. He was going to get away from there as quickly as possible. A moment more and he would slip the boat out of its hiding place behind the log, climb in and row as hard as he could for the city. The others would never catch him.

As he finished he noticed Stinger standing on the beach looking across the harbour. Jamie hated the very sight of him. He was a coward, only out to save his own skin and fill his pockets.

Suddenly he heard Stinger's urgent cry. "Darnby! Come here, quick!" The blond boy was pointing across the water. "Look … there … "

"What is it?"

"That mackinaw boat … it's the coppers and they're heading right for us!"

"You hain't serious?" Darnby's freckled face was flushed a deep red.

"I tell you it's the coppers. I'd recognize that boat anywhere. There's four men on the oars, and they're comin' fast."

Jamie bent down so he could see under the long dangling leaves of the willow. Some distance off was a big white rowboat with four long oars, two on each side, rhythmically dipping into the water. Another man was in the stern on the tiller. The boat was heading directly for their camp.

"Damn," Stinger spat. "Paddy and Bud must have squealed. What are we gonna do now?"

"We're going to move as quick as skinned lightning. The Toronto police won't catch a circus man like myself."

"All right, then. Let's go!"

A frantic panic seized them and the two started running in different directions.

"I'll get the loot," Darnby shouted.

"We don't have time! They're comin' too quickly!" Stinger was running down the beach shouting excitedly as he came. "Get the skiff out, Jamie. We've got to move!"

At first Darnby headed for the shore, but then he turned and splashed through the water. Jamie had pushed the boat free, then climbed over the side. Suddenly the man met the boat and launched himself into the bow so hard that the small skiff rocked dangerously from side to side.

"Wait," Stinger shouted. He had gone to Darnby's boat that was still on shore, grabbed the oars and with great splashes chased after them. The water was up to his waist as he scrambled into the stern.

"Row!" Darnby ordered in panic. "Row! We've got to get out of here before Moffat gets his beady eye on us!"

Jamie was already at the oars and with a couple of quick strokes he pulled them away from shore. Stinger put his oars into the fittings near the stern, sat down behind Jamie, and the two began rowing together.

Without even a mention of a plan they steered the rowboat west, skirting the north shore of the island as closely as they could, hoping the police had not noticed them.

Their luck seemed to hold. They rowed away from the camp and with each dip of the oars seemed farther away from trouble. Maybe they would escape completely.

But now Jamie didn't know what to think. Why was he trying to escape with the others? By attempting to get away he was showing the police that he was guilty.

He bent all of his strength into the oars. The stiffness in his back and arms from the last night's efforts gave him shooting pains at first, but soon he was rowing smoothly. Maybe if he stuck with the others he could get away and find Meg. She could help him sort out the mess.

"Row ... " Darnby was urging them on. "Row ... row ... row ... " he repeated at each stroke of the oars. It looked like they were going to get clear away. Just a little longer and the police couldn't possibly catch them.

They were rowing with their backs to the bow of the skiff, and Jamie did not take his eyes off the police boat a long way behind. The sun beat down out of a clear blue sky. The morning mist had disappeared and now there was a sharp glare off the surface of the water that made him squint painfully.

The boat skimmed along as sweat streamed from Jamie's forehead and splashed into his eyes.

"We're gonna get away." He heard Darnby give an excited laugh. "As you might say, Stinger, the coppers in this town are as thick as a post."

But just as he said this Jamie could see the rowers of the police boat pause, holding their oars in the air and drifting. They were close to the island, and they seemed to be studying the camp. Then, after a moment, the big mackinaw boat swung its bow to the west until it pointed directly at them, and the four long oars began rapidly beating the water once again.

"They've spotted us!" Jamie said with fresh panic.

"Row, damn it!" Darnby replied through gritted teeth. "We've got to get away!"

And Jamie pulled on the oars with even more effort. What was he going to do? If he was caught with Stinger and Darnby he was finished. He would be sent to the reformatory — maybe to the penitentiary.

"We can beat them coppers," Stinger muttered between strokes.

"But there are four of them on the oars," Jamie replied without pausing.

"Their boat's a lot heavier. We can beat them."

"Shut up and row," Darnby ordered. "We've got to win this race."

They were following the shore of the island, skimming past summer cottages, hotels, the lighthouse and a complex of makeshift wharves and boat houses. Other boats were out on the bay now, and people were leisurely setting their sails or readying their skiffs for a morning training session. They rowed past a two-masted yacht that was standing with its full summer sails set, waiting for a breeze to fill the slack canvas.

"They're getting closer," Jamie hissed between his clenched teeth.

"Be quiet," Darnby ordered, panic in his voice. "Row!"

Pain stretched down Jamie's neck, across his shoulders and knifed through the small of his back. He was beginning to flag. His arms ached, his hands were sore from blisters, but still he bent forward, dipped the oars into the calm surface of the water and stroked with all the power in his back, arms and legs.

"There's Moffat in the stern," Stinger said. "See him there? That copper. I hate him."

"We've got to get away! We're going to get away," Darnby replied. "Row, you two. Row!"

They passed the open mouth of Blockhouse Bay. A wrecked scow lay half submerged on the beach, its planking ripped away and the ribs exposed to the elements. A sculler slipped quickly past them, his narrow craft knifing through the calm waters. Skiffs and sailboats were everywhere, oblivious to the desperate race that was going on among them.

For a moment Jamie thought he should throw himself overboard and swim for shore. It wasn't that far away. He could see young boys and girls out playing on the beach without a care in the world. Maybe he could reach them. But maybe he couldn't ...

On the mainland Jamie could see the skyline of the west end of the city dominated by the huge dome of the provincial asylum. A train was making its way along the harbour front and vessels of all types were crowded into the docks. A big white side-wheeler backed out of the Yonge Street wharf and paused, motionless, as its bow swung towards the Western Gap.

A long spit of sand that was the very western part of the island was ahead of them. The lighthouse on the shore at Queen's Wharf was in plain view. The race was coming to an end. Through the Western Gap were the open waters of Lake Ontario with swells too large for their small skiff. Behind them the police were rapidly closing the gap. There was nowhere they could go.

Then Darnby was shouting excitedly. "There it is! That's how we're getting out of here!"

Jamie glanced around. He was pointing at the steamship that had pulled out of the Yonge Street wharf and now was heading towards them. It was an elegant white craft, over 250 feet long with a single smokestack sprouting out of its midships. As it got up its head of steam a huge black plume of smoke rose into the air. They could hear the engine thumping and the side-wheels slapping the water as it thrust the boat along. A clean shower sprayed up from the bow as it knifed through the water.

"That's our liberation, boys. Row … row like you've never rowed before. It's our only chance."

Behind them the police boat came on, not slackening its pace. Now they could make out the faces of the policemen clearly. Moffat was in the stern handling the tiller.

Darnby was on his feet waving his arms at the steamer. The captain was out on the bridge watching them with his binoculars. Suddenly there was a blast from the ship's whistle.

"They're going to do it, boys. That's what the signal means. We're home free. Victory's within our grasp!"

But Moffat was signaling to the steamer as well. Jamie could see the detective waving his arms. Then he held a megaphone to his mouth and shouted, "This is the police! I order you to stop! Darnby! You're under arrest."

They paid no attention. On came the steamer, not slackening its pace or varying its course one degree. With every dip of the oars it seemed to Jamie that they were thrusting themselves recklessly into the path of the ship where they could be crushed under its sharp bow or caught in the giant paddle wheels. But still they rowed.

"Stop!" Darnby shouted suddenly. "Let her drift."

Jamie turned. The tall sides of the white ship loomed up towards them. Water from the bow shot out in a high arching shower. The ship's engine pounded. The churning paddle wheels were deafening.

"Police!" they heard Moffat shout. "Stop … this is the police … !" But the rest was lost in the turbulence of the water and the thumping of the big steam engine.

The boat seemed to be bearing right down on top of them. Surely they would be crushed under the knife-like bow. The closer it came the louder the thumping and the greater the churning of the water.

Then the vessel was right on top of them. The bow passed a few feet away. Their skiff washed up with the huge wave and the side-wheel churned towards them. It would smash their boat into rubble and tear them to pieces. But suddenly the side-wheel stopped and the noise of the engine halted. Silence fell as the steamboat drifted.

"There! The ladder! Row, boys! We've got to make it!" Darnby shouted excitedly.

The ship's crew had lowered a rope ladder from the rail aft of the paddle wheel. The vessel was still drifting fast and Jamie and Stinger had to bend their backs into the oars to bring them alongside. Darnby reached a long way over the bow to catch the ladder, swaying and dancing as it dangled over the side.

"Stop!" Moffat was hollering. "This is the police!" The police boat was still more than a hundred feet away. The detective was shouting and waving his arms as the four policemen rowed as hard as they could.

Now Darnby had the ladder in his two hands. He swung over the bow of the skiff and with a guttural growl of victory he began scrambling up the rope ladder with the strength and agility of an acrobat. Just at that moment the steam engines suddenly began their thumping again and instantly the side-wheels started to turn. The noise was deafening, the water swirled as the current swept under the skiff. The steamboat was beginning to pick up speed.

Jamie dropped the oars and scrambled over the seats to the bow. Stinger clawed at him from behind, both of them desperate to grab the ladder.

Darnby was part way up the ladder now, but one foot still clung onto the bow of the boat. Jamie grabbed for his leg, but just as he reached him the current, sweeping back from the churning side-wheels, caught the skiff. Darnby's foot was wrenched out of the boat and into the water.

The boy lunged. Stinger's heavy body crushed against him as he reached over the bow, but they grabbed nothing but foam and spray.

Jamie collapsed, stunned that they had so narrowly missed escape. He could see Darnby climbing up the ladder and being helped over the rail by the two sailors. The steamboat was picking up speed now, heading out of the Western Gap to open water while he and Stinger watched helplessly.

The boy turned away just as the police boat swept up to them. Oars were pulled in and hands reached out to hold the skiff alongside.

"All right. You two are under arrest! Your race is over!"

CHAPTER 11

BRING them here," Moffat ordered, and Jamie and Stinger were forced out of the skiff and into the mackinaw boat by big policemen. There they were brought face to face with the detective.

"So it seems that you two have gone from bad to worse. First it was stealing rolls from a bread wagon, then you broke into a warehouse and now you try to escape from the police."

"We didn't do nothin'," came a surly reply from Stinger.

The detective's eyes opened wide in surprise. "Then why the race across the harbour?" He had on a cotton pullover with heavy pants and canvas shoes.

Stinger shrugged.

Moffat studied him carefully. "It seems like your friend Darnby purposely deserted you."

"What do you mean?"

"Just what I said. He got the two of you to row him all the way across the bay and then he scrambled aboard the side-wheeler and left you to us. He was only interested in saving his own skin."

"He couldn't help that. The boat started its engines before we could get to the ladder."

Moffat laughed. "You couldn't see because you were still on the oars, but once he grabbed the ladder he signaled to the sailors on the deck to leave."

"He did not!" Stinger protested.

"Look, I know your Mr. Darnby only too well. He says that you're going to be partners forever, but what he wants is to use boys like you to do his dirty work. The least bit of trouble and he leaves you to your fate and saves himself."

"I don't believe it."

"Are you any different, Stinger?" Now the detective's voice had a hard edge to it. "You've used this boy, Jamie, just like you've used Paddy and Bud and others in the past."

"Get off it, Moffat. You're tryin' to get me to talk but I ain't gonna tell you nothin'." The boy retreated into silence, his jaw clenched and his hands held tightly into fists.

Moffat paused for a moment, studying the boy with contempt. Then he turned to the other policemen. "Put the shackles on these two. They're going to jail."

Rough steel handcuffs were hauled out of a compartment in the bow of the boat and clamped on their wrists. A heavy chain joined them together. Jamie's arm was pinched painfully by the cold steel clamp. Then the men tied the skiff behind the police boat and began rowing back towards the city.

As Jamie sat there, his hands manacled, watching the city and the harbour, he felt stunned. Things had happened so quickly. But at the same time he knew that he was as guilty as Stinger or Darnby or the other two boys. Why had he been so stupid? What was he going to say to Meg? How would he tell his mother? What if he had to spend months or years in jail to pay for these crimes?

Suddenly Stinger jerked the handcuffs to get his attention. The boy was looking furtively about to check if anyone was listening. Then he whispered, "We don't say nothin' to the coppers, understand? We say nothin'."

"Stay away from me, Stinger."

"You listen or I'll split your head open."

But Jamie felt nothing but open defiance. "Leave me alone."

Suddenly Stinger lifted his manacled arms over his head as if to hit Jamie.

"Stop that!" Moffat ordered sternly from his seat at the tiller, and the street boy slowly lowered his hands.

But the look on Stinger's face was filled with venom. "Watch yourself, kid," he whispered. "Or I'll get you!"

But Jamie didn't care. What could Stinger do to him now?

The four policemen rowed them back to the central part of the harbour with long smooth strokes. Jamie was so lost in thought that he barely noticed the city slide past. The boat rounded the complex of wharves at the bottom of Yonge Street and slipped into the police dock.

"Out of the boat. Step lively, there, boys. We haven't got all day," Moffat ordered.

Stinger climbed out first and purposely yanked hard on the chain so that it pulled painfully on Jamie's arms. "Hey, watch it."

"You watch it, kid," snarled Stinger. "You watch out for everything."

"Settle down, you two."

Moffat sent the tall blond constable to send a telegram to Hamilton police. "That's the first stop for that side-wheeler," he explained. "Maybe they can catch Darnby as he disembarks."

The boat was tied up, and two of the policemen were stationed on either side of the prisoners with one walking behind. Moffat took the lead and they set off across the railway line and up Church Street. They walked swiftly, their shoes rhythmically pounding on the boardwalk while the chain that swung between Jamie and Stinger rattled with each step.

A matronly, prosperous-looking woman coming the other way stepped aside to avoid the procession. When she saw the boys' manacled hands a look of horror and disgust came over her face. A frock-coated merchant standing in the doorway of his shop studied them with a surly look. A couple of older men coming out of a tavern at King Street stared as they passed. It seemed to Jamie that the entire city of Toronto watched them being marched up Church Street like common criminals.

At King Street they passed a couple of newsboys that Jamie recognized. When the procession of police and prisoners clomped by them the boys' eyes opened wide. Soon every news vendor in town would know of their arrests.

At Court Street they swung west, climbed the stairs and went through the doors of the big police station.

Moffat went straight up to a uniformed officer sitting at a long wooden desk in the foyer. He paused and the two boys halted beside him.

"These two lads are to be held in jail," the detective announced.

"What are the charges?" asked the man behind the desk.

"Theft and escaping police custody. That will hold them until we can sort out all of the details."

The officer behind the desk took out a set of forms from his desk, wet his long pen with ink from the well, and took down the particulars: name, address, age, employment …

Stinger reacted angrily. "You got this stuff on me already."

"That's right. You've been through this routine more than once," Moffat replied. "Somehow you just don't seem to learn."

Jamie found it a chore giving all of the details as he stood with the manacles on his wrists. More than once he was ordered to speak up but finally he got through the ordeal.

When it was all over the boy cautiously asked, "Sir … do you think someone could find my sister Meg and tell her what has happened to me?"

"Your sister?"

"It's just that she doesn't know where I am and … and she'll be worried."

"You should have thought of that a long time ago." Moffat's hard eyes seemed to burn into Jamie for the longest time. Then he turned back to the officer behind the desk and gave another set of orders.

"I want these boys held in the cells downstairs. They are to be separated and not given a chance to talk to each other. Is that clear?"

"When are we gonna get to see the judge?" Stinger demanded.

"You'll get your chance, Stinger. All in good time. But first you'll have to talk to me."

"I ain't talkin' to no coppers. I told you that, Moffat. You ain't gonna get nothin' from me."

"We'll see about that, Stinger. We'll see."

Two burly jailers arrived. The police took off the handcuffs, and then the boys were taken away one at a time.

Stinger was taken first and the guard guided him along with a firm grip on the elbow. Jamie was taken in the other direction. They went through a doorway and began going down a spiral staircase into the recesses of the earth.

Down they went into the darkness. At the second landing they came to a small indentation in the wall where a candle flickered. The guard paused and finally released his grip on the boy's elbow. He lit another candle from the one burning, and then they proceeded again down the spiral staircase, down into the very depths of that dark place.

When they finally got to the bottom they found a heavy steel door. The guard opened it with a big brass key and motioned for Jamie to go inside. The flickering light showed a narrow passageway barely wide enough to walk along. Leading off it were a series of steel doors, each with an opening at chest level about one foot square, barricaded by a row of steel bars. The guard went down to the very end and opened the last door in the row. As he held up the candle so that light danced on the stone walls, his face looked gaunt and pale. "Inside," he ordered.

Cautiously Jamie peered through the dark, cavernous opening to the stone walls and floor of the cell. A steel wire bed was along one wall with no mattress on its frame, and a white enamel pot sat in the corner. The rest of the cell was empty.

Jamie hesitated.

"Get in, boy. I hain't got all day."

Stooping his head to avoid the low door frame, Jamie took one cautious step and then another. Suddenly he heard the steel door creak on its heavy hinges. He turned in panic just as the door caught him in the hip and shoulder, and he was pushed roughly inside. With a metallic clang the door slammed with a hollow echo that reverberated for seconds. The key rattled in the lock and then the light from the candle retreated down the passageway.

"Don't go ... please," Jamie begged in sudden panic, but the only reply was the heavy slam of the door out in the hallway and the sound of the key locking it securely.

Slowly Jamie turned and faced the emptiness of the cell. A catch came to his throat. Tears welled up in his eyes. He had been cast off. All he had was a cold grim police cell — a dungeon deep in the bowels of the earth.

Cautiously his hand went out and touched the cold roughness of the stone walls. He stepped into the centre of the room and felt the bed with his leg. One hand went out to touch the wall on one side and then the other reached out in the opposite direction. Slowly he began to explore his new environment.

It took him some time to realize that light was coming from somewhere. For a moment he thought he was deceiving himself, but after his eyes were used to the dimness, he could see that on the far wall, up near the ceiling, there was a slit about two inches wide and a foot long. Through that small gap came a shaft of weak light.

It was the sun. Jamie went up as close as he could to the small shaft of light, stood with his cheek up against the rough stone wall and looked up through the opening. For the longest time he leaned up against the wall. Then he moved across to the steel bed and sat down on the wire mattress. A calmness came over him. There was no point getting into a panic. It was up to the police to decide what would happen to him. All he could do was wait.

Noises flowed towards him. Overhead there was a series of scuffles as if people were walking on the heavy wooden floor. Somewhere far off he thought he heard the moans and cries of another prisoner, and then a *tap* … *tap* … *tap* … as if someone was trying to break the isolation of the place by this primitive means of communication.

He wondered what was happening to Stinger, Paddy and Bud. Where was Darnby at that very moment? And then he began thinking of his family and imagining what would be said when they learned he was in jail.

The boy was completely absorbed in his thoughts, staring blankly at the dim outlines of the stone walls for so long that he lost track of time. Suddenly, out in the hallway there was the noise of the steel door creaking open and then voices. Jamie sat up.

"It's the last door," came a male voice.

Candlelight flickered into the cell. "Jamie? Jamie, are you in there?"

It was Meg! The boy leapt to the door and pressed himself against the steel bars of the opening. "Meg! Thank God you've come!"

Her face was pale, her dark eyes cautious and afraid, and her mouth pulled into a tight frown. Jamie felt himself begin to cry.

"Jamie, are you all right?" Now she was beginning to sob. She pressed her face up against the bars, and Jamie pressed his face from the other side.

"I'm sorry, Meg. I'm sorry. Don't cry. Please don't cry. It's over now, I promise."

CHAPTER 12

MEG was allowed to stay only ten minutes and then the guard came to usher her out. And Jamie was left alone in the darkness again.

He wasn't sure how long he stayed there thinking and listening to the strange sounds that drifted into the dungeon. But finally there was a commotion out in the hallway. The heavy brass key rattled in the lock and the door swung open.

"Out you come," the guard ordered gruffly. "We hain't got all day."

Jamie groped towards the light. Compared to the dim darkness of the cell the candle seemed as bright as the sun. "Where am I going?" he asked.

"Upstairs."

They stumbled along the narrow corridor. The guard opened the heavy steel door and led him up the winding staircase. At the top the door was opened, and they were back in the main section of the police station. The sharp glare of light was blinding. As Jamie put his hand over his eyes the guard took him by the elbow and began steering him roughly along the hallway.

"I can walk by myself," the boy protested.

"You hain't gonna run on me, lad. I got me duty."

Jamie stumbled, but the guard didn't miss a step. He was taken down a maze of corridors. Then they stopped at a door. The man pounded on it twice and pushed it open.

"Your prisoner, sir," the guard announced as Jamie was thrust inside. Then the door was closed behind him.

Bright sunlight streaming through big windows seemed to scald Jamie's eyes. Two figures were sitting at a table, and after his eyes had adjusted to the light, Jamie saw that one was Detective Moffat, dressed in a conservative business suit, and the other was the young policeman who often accompanied him. He wore his blue uniform but had taken off his jacket and was sitting in shirt sleeves. The room was hot. Windows were open but there was hardly a breath of air.

"Come and sit down, Jamie," the detective said harshly and motioned to a straight-backed wooden chair standing in the shaft of sunlight.

Cautiously the boy stepped forward and eased himself into the seat. The two men studied him without a flicker of emotion. For the longest time there was not a word, not a movement, not a sound. Just the minute examination of every detail of the boy's appearance.

Finally Moffat drew a sheet of paper towards him and glanced at the writing scrawled there. "You're in real trouble, boy."

Jamie was beginning to perspire.

"We want you to tell the truth," the detective continued. "Maybe then things might go easier on you."

"What's going to happen to me, Mr. Moffat, sir?"

"That's up to the judge. Everything that has happened will be brought out. Then it's up to him to make a decision. So let's sort out the mess from the very beginning,"

"I don't know much about it, sir."

The detective leaned forward as if to hear better. "But you were involved in Stinger's gang."

"It wasn't really a gang."

"It was a group of boys who committed thefts and robberies. Isn't that right?"

"But I didn't take part in the thefts." The yellow sun was streaming through the window. Jamie felt so hot he was light headed.

Disbelief marked Moffat's face. "Are you telling me you were not part of the operation?"

Jamie felt confused. "Yes, sir ... no ... I mean, I didn't take part in the robberies."

"I find that hard to believe."

"But it's true. My job was to look after the boat."

Now the detective was annoyed. "I want to warn you, Jamie, that if you don't tell the truth things could go very hard on you. The courts don't like liars."

"But what I'm telling you is the truth."

"That's not what Stinger or the other boys tell us. We've got sworn statements from Paddy and Bud saying you participated in everything."

The sun was glaring into Jamie's eyes. Sweat was beading on his forehead. "They didn't tell me what was going on. They would go off to do their jobs and leave me looking after the skiff."

The detective glanced at his notes impatiently. "We have a police constable who will testify that you were involved with Stinger in stealing from a bread wagon. We have another who will swear that you were lurking in the alleyway next to a fur warehouse that was later found to be broken into. And we know for a fact that you, Jamie Bains, were the boy on the oars of the skiff last night who picked up Stinger just before he could be arrested. Not only do we know all of that, but this morning you tried to evade arrest by fleeing from the police." Now the detective leaned forward again. "Those are events we have firsthand knowledge about. We also have confessions from your accomplices that you were involved in every one of their robberies. The evidence is overwhelming. In my view you have been one of the central leaders of this gang."

Jamie buried his face in his hands. The heat and the pressure were making his head feel like it was going to explode. "But it wasn't like that, sir!"

"Look at the facts. You were involved in each one of the offences, amassing a great amount of loot. You arranged to have Bud and Paddy arrested so you would not have to share the spoils with them, and you planned your escape with Stinger and Darnby." He was pointing his finger at the boy now. "I think it is clear. You and Stinger and Darnby were the ring leaders of this whole operation."

The heat seemed to split Jamie's head open. "No … no … that's not the way it happened."

"Then where is the loot? Tell me that."

"I don't know. They never showed it to me. I don't even know what was stolen."

"You're lying. Not only are you an accomplished thief, but you try to lie to save your own skin."

Jamie held his throbbing head. His shirt was drenched with sweat. "You've got to understand, sir. I was involved, but I wasn't one of the ring leaders. I didn't even know what was going on. This morning, in fact, I was going to find Meg and give myself up to the police."

"Then why did you try to escape with the others?"

"I don't know. I don't know. It was so stupid." He was holding his head in his hands. "Everything you said was true, but I wasn't one of the ring leaders. I just waited with the boat and acted as lookout. I didn't do the stealing."

"I don't know, boy. This is a very serious case. We've got stolen property worth hundreds of dollars that we can't locate, and this man Darnby continues to be at large. We wired ahead to Hamilton police but he disappeared before they could find him. If we don't get the property back he might pick it up. Do you have any idea where he might be hiding?"

"No, sir. How would I know?"

"You were a friend of that Irishman Murphy and through him you brought Darnby into the gang. Now tell us where we might find him."

"I don't know."

"What do you mean you don't know?" The detective was shouting. "What you're saying is you won't help us. You're trying to cover up for Darnby and Stinger and yourself!"

"No! No! It's not like that!" The heat and the sun and the airless room were overwhelming. The relentless questioning tore at Jamie until he thought he would pass out.

"Take him away," Moffat said to the constable seated beside him. "I'm tired of hearing his lies and lame excuses."

The policeman wrenched him to his feet.

"What will happen to me?" Jamie asked weakly.

"Jail, boy!" the detective spat. "Tomorrow morning you will be in front of the judge and you can try your story out on him. Take him away!"

Jamie was swept out of the room by the policeman dragging on his arm, and he was taken down the hallway to where a jailer waited.

"Detective Moffat has ordered this boy to be locked up until tomorrow's court."

"Want him in a special cell or in the tank?"

"Makes no difference. He hasn't cooperated with us so there are no favours for him."

Jamie was taken into a huge cell. Two walls were made up of iron bars about three inches apart stretching from floor to ceiling. The dozen or more prisoners who occupied the place were ordered to stand back as the door was opened. Jamie was thrust inside and the door locked behind him.

A stale smell of urine and vomit greeted him. The floor was dirty and the windows smeared. The other inmates were a sorry-looking bunch. Some were in their early twenties but most were older. Many wore tattered clothing that made them look like beggars or the poorest class of worker. At first they were curious about this addition to their ranks but then most went on pacing back and forth in the cell or talking in small groups.

It took Jamie a minute before he spotted Stinger sitting in a corner, his legs stretched out and his arms folded in a hostile way. The big boy was the last person he wanted anything to do with, and he went down to the opposite end of the cell and sat down on the wooden floor. But Stinger had been waiting for him. Suddenly Jamie felt a sharp kick on the leg.

"Are they takin' you to court tomorrow?" the boy demanded.

Jamie nodded. "That's what Detective Moffat says."

"They ain't got nothin' on us." Stinger crouched down so he could whisper. He seemed to have forgotten their argument.

"He told me we were going to go to jail."

"He's crazy in the head. They ain't got one shred of evidence."

"Seems to me they have more than they'll ever need."

"He's just sayin' that to scare you, kid. They can't find the loot and they never will. As long as they don't have that they can't pin nothin' on us."

Jamie hated Stinger at that moment. "You're stupid. You pretend that you know everything but you don't know anything. Go away and leave me alone. You got me into this mess and all you can think about is the loot and saving your own skin."

"Shut up, kid." Stinger was on his feet now. His hands were doubled into fists and his jaw jutted out. He was big and powerful, at least five inches taller and thirty pounds heavier than Jamie. But in an instant Jamie was on his feet ready to defend himself. Now the other prisoners gathered around as if hoping for a fight.

Jamie was shouting. "I'm going to tell the world what a stupid person you are, Stinger!"

"Shut up or I'll … "

Suddenly one of the guards was in the cell and thrust himself between the two boys. He carried a truncheon a foot and a half long. "No fighting here!" he shouted. "You street rats keep your disputes to yourself." Then he pointed at Stinger. "Go down to the other end of the cell and stay there. And you stay at this end, kid. If there's any more trouble you'll have to deal with me." Reluctantly the two boys followed the orders.

The night was terrible. A couple of hours after Jamie had been put in the cell the evening meal was served. It consisted of a slice of stale bread and cold watery soup with a big lump of mashed potato floating in it. The food was about as appetizing as a mess of gruel, but Jamie ate every bit of it. He had not eaten all day and was ravenously hungry.

With nightfall gas lamps on the walls were turned on. They made a loud hissing sound and gave off a bright uncomfortable glare. A stuffy heat returned. The smell of sweat and urine became heavy and oppressive.

The men, packed into the cell like animals, moved about restlessly.

As the evening wore on, and the police out on their beats made arrests, the cell became even more crowded. Most of the newcomers were drunk. They would babble to themselves or shout obscenities at the guards. For a few minutes they would cause havoc, staggering about and getting into arguments, but soon they would stretch out on the floor and go to sleep.

The constant commotion of the place bothered Jamie, but his real concern was Stinger. Now he was wary of an attack and had to be on his guard.

That was the main reason he stayed in his corner for so long, but after awhile he got stiff from sitting on the hard floor and joined the others pacing back and forth. It was then that Jamie discovered that Stinger had curled up and gone to sleep. He began to feel a little more relaxed.

Finally the boy was so exhausted he couldn't stay awake any longer. He climbed into his corner beside a drunken man wheezing and coughing in his sleep. He closed his eyes and drifted off. When he awoke it was morning.

They had eaten a breakfast of cold lumpy porridge when a guard came to the door of the cell and called out in a loud voice, "Here is the list of men going to court. Get in line and step lively. The judge won't be kept waiting."

The list included both Jamie and Stinger. They joined the others and were marched off to another part of the building that housed the courts. There they had to sit and wait on hard benches for the longest time, but finally their names were called and they were ushered into the courtroom by a blue-coated police constable.

It was a big room. The black-robed judge sat up on a raised platform behind an elaborate mahogany desk. A number of assistants busied themselves with paperwork. A Union Jack hung from a standard, there was a Canadian crest on the wall and a painting of a young Queen Victoria. Lawyers and police officers huddled in groups whispering. In the audience were a couple of dozen spectators listening attentively.

Jamie suddenly saw how he must appear to those in the courtroom. His thatch of brown hair was uncombed, his hands and face grubby, and his clothes dirty and unkempt from days of selling newspapers, sleeping out in the open, and the hot uncomfortable night in the police cell.

Things happened quickly. The charges against them were read in a rapid-fire voice by one of the court clerks. The only thing that made sense to the boy were their names and, " … you did violate the criminal code in that you stole property from the Canada Fur Company on Sherbourne Street. "How do you plead? Guilty or not guilty?"

"Not guilty," Stinger called out defiantly.

"And how do you plead, Jamie Bains? Guilty or not guilty?"

The boy was confused. "I don't know, sir. Like … I didn't steal anything."

The judge leaned forward and peered at him over the top of his wire spectacles. He had a thick crop of white hair with long bushy sideburns. "But how do you plead, boy? Guilty or not guilty?"

"I … I'm not sure, sir."

"All right. We'll put it down as a not guilty plea."

"If I can help the court, Your Worship." Detective Moffat stood at a desk a few feet from the judge's raised platform. He was dressed in a neat blue suit. "The police are not prepared to go ahead with the trial of these boys at this time. We have a warrant out for the apprehension of an accomplice named Darnby, and we have not completed our investigation. We would like to delay the trial for one week to see if we can apprehend Darnby so that we can bring him to trial at the same time."

The judge was nodding. "That's reasonable. I will remand the case for one week. These two accused will be held in custody until that time."

"Sir … sir … please, sir!" Jamie swung around quickly to find the familiar voice. It was Meg. She was standing at a wooden fence-like barrier dividing the court from the spectators. A court officer rushed up and was trying to silence her. Voices were rising.

"Order … order in the court!" the judge said with annoyance.

"Please, sir, let me speak. I am Meg Bains, the sister of one of these boys."

The judge took off his glasses. "All right, I'll let you speak," he said sternly. "But I hope this pertains to the matter at hand."

The courtroom became silent as Meg gathered herself together. She spoke with a steady, calm voice.

"Sir, I am Meg Bains, the sister of Jamie, the young boy in the dock. I would like to ask you not to send him to jail, but let him come home with me. My brother is only twelve years old, sir. I will make sure that he comes back for his trial."

Detective Moffat got to his feet. The judge indicated he could speak by a nod in his direction. "Your Worship, in the view of the police Jamie Bains was very much involved in these offences. He was one of the ring leaders, and we would like him held in custody."

"Very well, request denied. He will be held in custody for one week."

"But, sir, he's just ... " Meg pleaded.

The judge hammered his gavel. "Order! You will not interrupt my court. These two boys will both be held in custody for one week, and then we will hold the trial. Take them away."

It was as Jamie was being led out of the courtroom by the officer that he thought he caught sight of Murphy, the big Irishman, heading out of the spectators' gallery. It looked just like him, but he couldn't be certain. In a moment the man was gone.

CHAPTER 13

WHEN the morning court session was over, the police shackled the six prisoners together who were to be taken to the city jail and led them through a back door to a black van marked "Toronto Municipal Police." Once they were inside two constables armed with long billy clubs climbed in after them, the door was locked, and then with a sharp jerk the team of horses clomped off through the street at a rapid pace.

The only window in the van was a small opening in the door covered with iron mesh. Jamie tried to peer out at the passing streets to see where they were going but could only catch glimpses of buildings and the pale blue sky. What was going to happen to him now? Part of him no longer cared.

For fifteen minutes or more the van jolted through the streets and then Jamie suddenly saw a big stone structure through the window.

"What's that?" he asked.

"The old city jail," one of the police officers replied. "That'll be your cozy home for the next week."

Jamie remembered seeing the fortress-like building that dominated the eastern end of the harbour. It was massive. The central part was a four-storey octagon with a tower and weather vane on top. Two huge wings radiated out from it with rows of small, half-circle barred windows. It looked like a grim, forbidding place.

The van was driven into a court on the ground floor of the central part of the building, and the back door was opened. The prisoners climbed out, their chains rattling, and were ushered into a room where the door was locked behind them. Only then were the shackles removed.

A top-hatted man with a long, black cutaway coat came in. He had a neatly trimmed greying beard and carried a silver-headed walking stick.

"Quiet … quiet now," barked one of the guards. "This is Major Clarke, the warden of the jail. He would like to say a few words."

"I hardly feel I should welcome you to Toronto city jail." The warden spoke in the rounded, cultured accent of an upper-class Englishman. "This is not a hotel. We have strict rules here and you will obey them or take the consequences. I urge you to follow the one major rule of this place and that is to obey the directions of the guards. If you do not, then you will live to rue the day you ended up in a place like this. Do I make myself clear?" The warden abruptly turned and walked out of the room swinging the walking stick as he went.

"Cruel. That's what he is," murmured an older man beside Jamie. "A real cruel one."

"Order now," said the guard. "You're going to have lunch and then you will join the other inmates to witness a disciplinary action. There you'll see what the warden was talking about."

It was a meal of soup, a potato and a slab of fatty bacon that Jamie could hardly touch. The guards insisted on complete silence while they ate and constantly urged them to hurry up.

When they were finished they were taken into a large open space, the ground floor of one of the wings. Three sets of tiered walkways went all the way around the room. The dozens of doors that led off the tiers were the entrances to the cells.

In that room they joined the rest of the prison population of about one hundred men. Jamie spotted Paddy and Bud on the opposite side of the crowd and would have joined them except that all of the prisoners were standing quietly as if waiting for something to happen. For the moment he had to content himself with catching their eye and exchanging fleeting smiles.

They had not been there more than a minute when a young man was brought in. His hands were shackled together and he was naked from the waist up. He was taken to the centre of the big open space and his wrists were tied to a long pole over his head. Men shifted restlessly as they saw what was about to happen. Murmurs of subdued anger spread through the crowd.

Then the warden came through a door, swinging his walking stick aggressively. With him was a big man carrying a long whip.

"I don't want to see this," Jamie whispered.

"It's a strong stomach you need for this place, boy," a man next to him muttered.

Then the warden addressed the crowd in his clear, refined voice. "This man has been sentenced to be flogged with ten strokes of the lash for verbally abusing one of the guards. I want everyone here to watch carefully because this is what will happen if you disobey our rules." He nodded to the guard carrying the lash and the beating began.

Jamie buried his face in his hands, but he could not block out the whistling of the whip, the sickening sound as it struck human flesh, and the screams of the prisoner. Again it happened: the whistling, the sharp crack and the piercing scream.

Ten strokes of the lash. Jamie counted each one of them with his hands covering his eyes before he dared look up. The man's back was criss-crossed with red welts. Blood oozed out of the wounds. He looked like he was about to lose consciousness.

"Let this stand as a warning," the warden announced to the men. Then he turned and walked out the door, his stick swinging in a military fashion. The guards cut down the beaten man and carried him away.

"Jamie! Jamie! You're here!" It was Paddy and Bud. The three of them gave each other tight hugs. "How did you get here?" "What happened?"

The boy was about to explain when Stinger loomed up beside them. The three boys stopped talking.

"Have you guys squealed to them coppers?" he snarled.

Paddy looked around uneasily. "They caught us, Stinger. We had to say something."

"Didn't I tell you that you don't say nothin' to the law? I've got a mind to break your head, Paddy."

"Leave him alone," Jamie interrupted. "Moffat told me he got a statement out of you, Stinger. I bet you were singing away to try and save your own skin."

"I didn't do nothin' like that! I'm no squealer!"

"You're only interested in saving yourself, Stinger."

"Shut up, kid!"

They were shouting now. Other prisoners were gathering to watch. Suddenly Stinger's fist swung hard at Jamie, but the boy was too fast for him. He ducked, and the fist only struck air.

"Jamie, don't fight! They'll beat you," Paddy pleaded. "You saw what happened."

"I'll get you, kid!" Stinger murmured between clenched teeth, as two guards approached quickly. Sullenly he withdrew across the courtyard to stand with another group of prisoners while the three friends began to talk in earnest.

"What happened?" Bud asked. "Why are you so angry at Stinger?"

Jamie began to explain what had happened. "The morning after you were arrested, Stinger, Darnby and I were at your camp and the police closed in. Darnby managed to get away but they got Stinger and me."

"What's Detective Moffat going to do with us?" asked Paddy timidly.

"Jail. That's what he says."

Bud was close to tears. "We can't go to jail, Jamie. I can't stand this place with the beatings and the … "

"It'll be worse for us," Paddy added pathetically. "We've been up in front of the judge before."

"Isn't there some way we can get out of here? I can't stand it." Paddy put his arm around Bud, but the boy was crying.

Jamie was frightened, too. How was he ever going to get through a week of staying in that awful jail? If they got sentenced to prison they would spend months, even years in places like this.

A whistle was blown somewhere and a guard barked out orders. "All right, you men line up. You're going back to your cells. New prisoners are to wait here."

"Jamie, you've got to help us," Bud pleaded. "If we get out of here we will never break another law. Never. But we've got to get out!"

The two boys went to join the line of men with sad faces. Then they were led up the stairways. Steel doors creaked open and then slammed shut with an echoing sound that shook the building to its core.

Jamie was led with the new prisoners high up to the third tier and locked into an empty cell. He slumped on the wire mesh cot that hung out from the wall without even glancing around. The sounds of slamming steel doors reverberated through the stone prison as the inmates were locked into their narrow cubicles.

How could they ever get out of this place? The judge was bound to find them all guilty.

Now he was pacing back and forth. Heavy limestone walls surrounded him. The rough floors rasped at his feet. The door was a solid sheet of heavy steel with a small slot barely big enough to peek through. A small, barred window in the shape of a half moon let in a soft light.

Jamie could just reach up and grasp a steel bar in either hand. With effort he pulled himself up until he could see out the window. He was high up on the top floor of the prison that looked over the east end of the harbour. White billowy clouds were drifting in a soft, pale-blue sky. The islands formed a long green slip of land with a line of pale brown sand beach at its margins. Beyond lay the deep open water of Lake Ontario.

He could see the yachts and skiffs out in the water drifting without purpose. A two-masted schooner breached the Eastern Gap and Jamie watched the sailors strip the sails as the vessel was brought into a wharf. Side-wheelers manoeuvred into their berths, sending up tall columns of black smoke. He could even see the long stone jetty that came out from the mouth of the Don River and began to dream about that day when he had gone up the river with the boys to swim.

As he looked out at the island it occurred to Jamie that the stolen property must still be there. Darnby had gone off to hide it on the night of the rainstorm, and they had left in too much of a rush the next morning to get it.

Then it hit him. How could he have been so stupid? Moffat wanted to recover the property. Maybe he could find it for them.

He dropped from the window so that he could concentrate. If he helped the police find the property and return it to its rightful owners then maybe the judge could be convinced to go easier on them. Yes, that was it. He had to help the police recover the property.

In the late afternoon there was a rattling on his cell door as a key was inserted into the lock. As it swung open a guard called out, "Jamie Bains. You've got a visitor."

Meg waited for him in a long narrow room with visitors on one side of a heavy wire mesh fence and prisoners on the other. She was filled with questions about how he was getting on, but Jamie was too excited to talk about details.

"Meg, you've got to go and find Detective Moffat."

"Why?"

"I've got a plan. Maybe I can get out of here."

"But the judge and the police … "

"If I can find the loot, Meg. Don't you see? If I can find the stolen property then maybe the judge will go easier on us."

"Do you know where it is?"

"I think so. Tell Moffat that I think I can find it."

"But what if he won't listen?"

"He's got to listen. He's just got to believe me. Paddy and Bud and I have to get out of this place. Just try and find Moffat. Please."

After the evening meal he was locked up in his cell again. At first he paced back and forth in his narrow cubicle, worrying about what was going to happen. Would Moffat come? Would he listen to Meg? Would the stolen property be there?

As nightfall approached Jamie boosted himself up to look through the window again. A beautiful sunset brightened the western sky, casting gold and red into the fluffy clouds. Out on the bay sailboats were taking the last tack of the evening before heading home. A train filled with passengers pulled out of the station along the waterfront. Slowly the darkness gathered. Gas lamps along the waterfront were turned on, the sun made its last glorious display, and the night was upon them.

Jamie lay on his bunk in the darkness. He was tired but his excitement would not let him sleep. Sounds of the prison came drifting up to him. Moans of men, too long confined, hung in the air. Once there was a piercing scream that echoed through the tiers before finally easing away. But mostly it was the oppressive quiet of the place — a silence as heavy as the stones from which the prison was built.

It was right after breakfast that Moffat arrived. Jamie was ordered into an interrogation room and found the detective with his police officer partner.

"Your sister tells me you've been thinking a little since coming into this place," he said flatly.

"Yes, sir. I think I can find the stolen property."

"Really? Why did it take you so long to remember?"

"I didn't think it was important."

"That's hard to believe. Where is it?"

"Over at the camp on the island. When we spotted your police boat that morning of the chase, we left in such a hurry that Darnby didn't have time to get the sack of stuff."

"Do you know exactly where it is?"

"Not quite, but I think I can find it."

Moffat stared at him coldly. "Is this why you've brought me all the way down to this prison?"

"The stuff has to still be there, sir."

"Why should I believe you?"

"But it's true." Jamie was pleading with him now.

Slowly the detective folded his arms without taking his eyes off the boy. "I think you're just telling a story, boy."

"No!"

"You've just cooked up this line to try and find some way out of this place."

"No! It's not like that." Jamie was almost crying. "Please believe me, sir. Please!"

"You're a criminal at heart, boy. I know your kind. Just a common criminal. Well, you can rot in here for all I care. Maybe then you might learn that here in Toronto we don't put up with this sort of thing."

"No, sir. Please!" Big tears were flowing down Jamie's face.

"Guard ... !" Moffat was calling. "Guard. Take this boy back to his cell." He turned to look at the weeping prisoner. "You'll never put one over on us, Jamie Bains," he shouted. "Never!"

CHAPTER 14

A cold chill settled on Jamie as he was ushered back into his cell by the two big guards. There was no hope now that he would ever be released from that dismal cold place. He was doomed. Finished.

When the call for the noon meal was shouted along the prison tiers, and the cell door thrown open, Jamie lay on his cot without moving. But he didn't even have the freedom to do that. A guard rousted him out and he was forced to go down to the exercise yard and join the others in the mess hall.

The meal consisted of soup, bread, potatoes and a thin slice of salt pork washed down with big cups of black tea. The food was cold and tasteless. Everything was served on tin plates and eaten with sour-tasting spoons. Jamie found he couldn't swallow a thing.

Absolute silence was maintained throughout the meal by a burly guard who stood at the head of the table. Jamie was by far the smallest and youngest of their group but a lot of the prisoners were in their teens and early twenties. Some looked restless, others angry, but most were cowed and defeated by the place.

They were given no longer than ten minutes to eat. At a signal from the guards, one at a time the rows of men picked up their plates and spoons and carried them to big barrels near the kitchen where they were washed by a detail of prisoners. Then they were marched out to the big room again. For the next half hour they would be allowed to exercise.

"Jamie ... Jamie! We're over here." Paddy and Bud were glad to see him.

"We heard you saw Moffat this morning," said Paddy.

"How did you know that?"

"In a prison you get to know everything. What was it all about?"

Jamie glanced uneasily around. "I tried to get Moffat to take me over to the island to look for the loot. I figured if I could find the stuff the judge would go easier on us. But he wouldn't do it."

"So you're out there helpin' the coppers put the finger on the rest of us." It was Stinger. He had come up quietly behind them and had overheard the last bit of their conversation. He spoke so the guards would not hear him but he spat the words out angrily. "I knew you was a rat from the first time I saw you, Jamie. Just a slime-ball rat lookin' for a chance to sell out your brothers."

"You're the rat, Stinger," said Paddy. "At least Jamie's trying to help us get out of this mess."

"Get out of it? Finding the stuff would only help Jamie. The rest of us would rot in here. Besides, you'll never find the loot. Darnby is smarter than all the rest of you put together. You'll never find where he's hidden the stuff."

"Do you know where it is?" asked Paddy.

"I ain't sayin'."

"Then you're stupid," announced Paddy bitterly. "You're even stupider than I thought, Stinger."

"Darnby's the one who's going to win from all this," Jamie said. "He's going to get the loot and walk away scot free while the rest of us rot in jail."

"Well, good," said Stinger. "Better that he gets the stuff than them coppers. I'd rather rot in prison than sing to them." He walked abruptly away.

The next morning at breakfast a guard read out the names of all those prisoners who were going to court. Jamie's name was among them, along with Bud, Paddy and Stinger. They waited behind in the exercise area as the others were locked up. Then Jamie tried to explain to the guard that there must be some mistake.

"We were in the court just two days ago, and the judge put off our case for a week."

"Your name's on the list. That means you have to go to court," replied the guard and he walked away.

"They're going to do us in," Paddy whispered with a worried look. "They must have decided to send us to prison right away."

"But there must be a mistake. They were going to try and catch Darnby."

"Maybe they figure they don't need him."

"That's not what Moffat said."

Paddy looked dejected. "He's changed his mind. It's all over for us."

Bud had big eyes. "I'm scared. They're gonna send us away for a long time."

"It can't be." But the more Jamie thought of it the more it looked like it was true.

They were led to a room where shackles were fixed to their wrists and a heavy chain was strung from prisoner to prisoner.

Stinger was about to be chained to Jamie when he protested, "I'm not gonna be chained to that rat."

"What's wrong, Stinger," said the guard. "Found someone even worse than yourself?"

"Do you think we're going to be tried today?" Jamie asked the older boy.

"That's right, kid. You and me and the others will be goin' to prison together. That's gonna give me a nice long time to get at you. So watch out, 'cause once you're in prison you ain't got a chance against me."

The prisoners were crowded into the van, policemen climbed in behind them, the door was locked, and they were off. Jamie could hear his heart beat. It was really going to happen: the trial, the conviction and the sentence to prison. It was over and there was nothing he could do.

When they arrived the shackles were taken off and they were crammed into a stuffy room behind the court to wait their turn. It was mid-morning before the four of them were ushered through doors and found themselves standing in the dock of the courtroom. There was a tense hush over the place. The black-robed judge with his white hair and spectacles studied documents. Detective Moffat stood with a bevy of lawyers, officials and policemen without even looking at them.

Panic struck Jamie like a knife in the stomach. Where was Meg? He searched among the courtroom spectators trying to find her. Had they not told her about the changed court date? Would he be sent to prison without her even being there?

Now Detective Moffat was on his feet talking in a calm, clear voice. "Your Worship, these four boys appeared in court earlier in the week and have been held in the old city jail awaiting trial. We have been attempting to apprehend another individual involved in the case, an adult by the name of Darnby, but he continues to elude us. What I would suggest to the court is that we release these boys until the day of the trial."

Jamie couldn't believe his ears. Release them?

"This is most unusual, Mr. Moffat. These are serious charges. What assurances do we have that these boys will not get involved in further offences?" The judge peered at him over his glasses.

"Your Worship, Mr. Jones is here from the Newsboys' Home. I have talked to him and he is willing to accept responsibility for the supervision of the two youngest boys. What I would suggest is that the court order them into his custody. The other two could go free."

The judge shuffled through his papers. "What about Jamie Bains? He's only twelve years old according to these papers."

"I have talked to his sister, Your Worship. She has assured me that she will look after her brother and will bring him back for the next court appearance."

For the first time Jamie spotted Meg standing at the rail of the bar. The judge saw her as well. "Are you Miss Bains?"

"Yes, sir."

"I remember. Are you willing to take responsibility for your brother?"

"Yes, sir. I'll look after him. There'll be no problems."

"Very well, then. If the Crown is satisfied, Mr. Moffat, so am I." The judge rattled off more legal jargon and signed some papers before looking up. "You can go now boys, and you can thank Detective Moffat for your freedom. All I can say is that you'd best not be involved in any more trouble or there will be grave consequences."

Jamie could barely believe his ears. Freedom! It came as a complete shock. A court official swung open the gate of the dock. For a moment Jamie hesitated as if he still couldn't believe his good luck, but he saw Meg smiling, tears on her cheeks, and he rushed out to her.

The boys milled around, hugging each other happily. "Outside," the detective whispered. "The court has other business."

In the corridor Jamie was the first to speak. "We can't thank you enough, Mr. Moffat. To get out of that prison … "

Bud was crying. Paddy was holding onto him and saying, "Thank you, Mr. Moffat, sir. We'll be good. You'll see."

"You'll have to be. You heard what the judge said." The detective looked very serious.

Paddy and Bud went off to talk to Mr. Jones from the Newsboys' Home while Jamie and Meg chatted excitedly. Stinger was in the corridor but not part of the group. Jamie noticed him slip behind a crowd of people and then glance furtively back towards them. A moment later he was at the door and gone.

CHAPTER 15

MOFFAT had work to do and he went back to his office, leaving Meg and Jamie to wander outside. In a few minutes Bud and Paddy joined them along with Mr. Jones.

"You must be back at the home by six tonight," the superintendent reminded the two young boys. Then he hurried away, leaving the group gathered in the shade on the front steps of the police station.

The jail had left the boys grubby. Their clothes were dirty and their faces and hands had grime ground into them, but still they were in good spirits. Bud skipped around happily and Paddy couldn't help smiling.

"I can't believe we're out of jail," said Paddy. "It feels so good."

Jamie nodded. "I was sure we were going to be sent to prison."

"Who knows?" added Meg seriously. "It may still happen." She looked tired and concerned. "The judge won't be happy when he hears all of the evidence. I'm not sure what we can do, but Jamie had the idea that if he could find the stolen loot and get it back to its owners things might go easier on everyone. I still think that's a good idea."

Paddy was nodding. "Why don't we all go over to the island and have a look? Bud and I have to get some of our stuff, anyway."

The four of them began walking down Church Street towards the harbour. On the way they stopped at a small store to buy some groceries. When they came out Meg and Jamie walked behind the other two and she explained what had been happening while he was in jail.

"I lost my job at the warehouse, Jamie. I had to miss so much time from work to go and see you and attend court that the boss finally let me go. He said he needed someone more reliable."

"Meg, that's awful. It's all my fault. What are we going to do?"

"I don't know. This morning before court I moved out of our room and stored our stuff down at the train station. I figured we had to save what little money we had left."

Jamie felt terrible. "It's been all my fault, Meg." He thrust his hands deep in his pockets and hunched his shoulders as he walked along.

"Don't be silly, Jamie."

"No, it's all my fault. I should have listened when you said I should get a job."

His sister smiled and linked her arm through his. "But then I shouldn't have lectured you so much."

Jamie squeezed her arm.

At the harbour the sun glared off the surface of the water. There was not a breeze. The sails of the boats hung limp, and the water hardly stirred a ripple. The hot breath of the day made the sweat soak through their clothes.

They went onto the dock where the police kept their boats and searched for the boys' skiff, but it was nowhere to be found. Paddy went up to a man who appeared to be on duty and asked about their boat.

"The one that was here for a couple of days? Another lad came about fifteen minutes ago. He claimed that boat was his, and he took it."

"A big boy?" Jamie asked. "Blondish hair? About sixteen years old?"

"Yes, that's right. You probably can still see him." The man walked to the end of the dock. "Yes, there he is. About half a mile to the west. He's following the shore line."

It was Stinger, all right. Despite the distance, the shape of the skiff, the boy's blond hair and his rough blue shirt were all clearly recognizable. He was putting his back into the oars, and the boat was moving along at a good clip.

"Where can he be going?" Jamie asked as he looked across the water.

"Who knows?" Paddy replied.

They thanked the man for his trouble and then walked back to the end of the dock. Paddy sat down on a wooden post and folded his arms. He looked defeated. "What are we going to do now? Stinger's even got our boat. He's got everything."

Jamie put his hand on the boy's shoulder. "Darnby had a boat that he took over to the island. It must still be there. We can use that until you get your own back."

"Yeah, maybe." Paddy got to his feet. "Sure, why not?"

They walked down to the harbour to the wharf where the steamers took passengers across to the island. Meg bought fares for them all and in a few minutes they were out on the waters of the bay again.

Once the steamer was out on the water Jamie left the others to climb up to the top deck and looked west. Stinger was a long way away now, barely distinguishable in the bright glare of the sun, but it looked like he was still bending into the oars.

Where could he be going? Why had he been so anxious to slip away from the rest of them? He must have gone directly down to the harbour, got the boat and started rowing. He seemed to know exactly what he was going to do, as if he had planned it out long in advance. But why?

"What are you thinking about, Jamie?" The boy jumped in surprise. Meg had come up on him from behind.

"Why do you think Moffat let us go?" the boy asked. His blue eyes were troubled.

"I don't know for sure." Meg looked across the water at the approaching island. "Maybe he figured that jail wasn't good for you."

"Maybe, but that just doesn't sound like Moffat."

When they disembarked they had a walk of half a mile or more to their camp on the east end of the island. At first they went past summer cottages and hotels. People were sunning themselves on the beach and children played, splashing through the water, building sand castles and swimming. These were affluent families whose money could buy a carefree, happy summer for their children.

The four young people walked along a dusty road until they got to the end of a narrow trail through a marshy, reed-infested part of the island. Just before the camp a thicket forced them down to the beach, and they even had to wade through the water to get around some overhanging willow trees. The boys were dressed for this type of hike, but Meg had to be careful not to get her dress soaked or a hem caught. By the time they got to the camp it was well past noon and everyone was hungry.

They had bought a loaf of bread and they each had a slice along with a chunk of cheese. Bud searched around the camp while the others rested on the embankment.

"Darnby's boat is here," he called. "But there are no oars."

"We've got a spare set in behind the lean-to," Paddy replied.

Bud looked around some more and then came and sat on the bank with the others. "Looks like everything is the way we left it."

"Then the stolen goods have to be here somewhere," Jamie added. "They couldn't have just disappeared."

When they had finished eating the four of them went to look at the camp. Jamie stood by the burned out fireplace. "The night of the rainstorm Darnby and Stinger sat around the fire looking at the loot. Then as I came close Darnby closed up the sack and headed in the direction of that big willow tree. When he came back he was empty handed. He wasn't gone more than a minute."

"Then it's still got to be over there," said Paddy heading toward the tree. The other three followed behind.

They walked along a narrow, well-beaten path, through thick underbrush. On one side it was wet and swampy while on the other tightly packed trees were crowded together. A big weeping willow, easily three feet in diameter, lay right ahead.

Jamie stopped for a moment and looked all around. It had to be there somewhere, but where? Where would Darnby hide a sack like that?

At the tree they looked up into the branches and poked around the roots but found nothing. Then, systematically, they began searching the surrounding area. Paddy covered every inch of the thicket while Jamie and Bud plodded through the marsh. Meg went beyond the tree to search through an area of thick bulrushes. But none of them could find a trace of the canvas bag.

"It's hopeless," Jamie said finally. "Looks like we'll never find it." He went back to the beach and sat in a patch of sunshine.

The others gradually extended the area of their search, and when they found nothing, they went back to the big tree and started again. But the longer they looked the more discouraged they became, and one by one they each gave up and joined Jamie at the beach.

Paddy was the last. "Maybe Darnby's already been back to get it," he suggested.

Meg nodded. "It's possible. He's smart and he sure wouldn't leave valuable property lying around in a hiding place. What was in the bag, anyway?" Meg asked.

"Furs and other stuff," answered Paddy.

"Furs?" said Jamie, sitting up suddenly. "I didn't know it was furs. The night you got caught — the night of the big storm — did you go back to the fur warehouse?"

"Yeah." Paddy was stretched out on the beach. "Stinger was determined to go back because he knew there was a lot of valuable stuff in there. But when he came out there were coppers everywhere. We ran like scared rabbits, and, well ... you know what happened."

Jamie shook his head. "Stupid. That Stinger is so stupid."

"Yeah, well, maybe we were all stupid."

They talked for a long time, sitting in the hot sun. Then the three boys washed their clothes in some strong lye soap they had in the camp, and hung them up to dry on the bushes. Afterwards they swam and sunned themselves.

Meg watched the boys from the bank. It was good to see them so carefree and happy.

"Why can't it always be like this?" Jamie asked no one in particular. "Sunning ourselves, swimming, having a good time. It's perfect." But no one bothered to reply. The boys knew that they had to struggle to make a living, and no one expected it to be any different.

By mid-afternoon the two younger boys said they had to be going. They had a six o'clock curfew and Mr. Jones was strict.

"Would you mind if Meg and I stayed in your camp for a few days?" Jamie asked, and he explained how Meg had had to get out of their room.

"Sure," said Paddy, and Bud agreed. "We can't stay here ourselves, anyway."

"Good ... thanks. Come on. I'll row you across to the city."

The boys put on their clean clothes, already dried from the sun, packed their stuff in the boat and Jamie took them across the harbour. By the time he got back Meg had cooked a supper of eggs and bacon over the open fire. They ate it with thick pieces of bread washed down with mugs of tea. Afterwards they cleaned up their plates, tidied the camp and then went for a ride in the harbour in Darnby's skiff.

For the first time in days Jamie felt clean and almost relaxed. The hush of the evening was beginning to gather. Now the water was still and the heat of the day began to rise. As the boat drifted with each pull of the oars, the boy looked at the scene.

The city with its spires, domes and smokestacks rose gently from the lake front, but what interested him was the grey jail that dominated the east end of the harbour. From that distance the small half-circle windows were like tiny dots on the surface of the walls. It was hard for him to believe that just the night before he had pulled himself up to look out one of those windows to catch sight of the bay and daydream about freedom.

They rowed in silence for a long time and then Jamie asked, "What are we going to do now, Meg?"

"We have to find work, and we have to get you out of this trouble."

"Maybe we will both have to go back to selling papers."

Meg shook her head. "Perhaps we should just find somewhere else to live. I think the real reason I lost my job is because the owner of the warehouse found out you were in jail. Maybe we'll have to move."

As they drifted a steamer came in through the Eastern Gap churning the quiet waters of the harbour with its enormous side-wheels. Sailing boats were heading for their berths. A cargo schooner slipped silently out into the lake.

The sun was setting lower on the horizon. Red clouds stretched halfway over the sky, promising another day as hot and beautiful as the one that was just dying. A pale half-moon cast a cool white light. Jamie loved that place. He would miss it if they moved.

"What's not fair is that Stinger and Darnby are going to get away with all this," said the boy.

"We'll see."

"But where can they be? That's what I'd like to know."

CHAPTER 16

MOST of the night it was hot, and Meg and Jamie slept half in and half out of the lean-to. Towards dawn it got cool. In their sleep they snuggled together under the rough blankets, their bodies curled up to keep warm and their heads buried under the covers.

As the sun cracked over the horizon Jamie woke up. He pulled the blankets off his face and looked out at the day. Through the leaves and branches slanted shafts of sunlight that caught the rising mists, making it look as if the trees themselves were smoking.

The boy got up and pulled on his clothes. He walked down to the water's edge and stood, watching the mist rise as the sun warmed the air. In a couple of minutes he could clearly see the city and watch the traffic in the harbour.

"You're up early, Jamie," Meg smiled. She was already fully dressed.

"I couldn't sleep anymore. I wish I knew what the judge was going to do."

"You'll find that out soon enough. There's nothing you can do about it now. Come on, let's have something to eat."

Jamie got out the loaf of bread, cut off a couple of pieces with a sharp knife and then sliced slabs of Cheddar cheese. They sat in front of the lean-to chatting as they ate while the day wore on.

They had been up for a couple of hours, maybe more, when Jamie walked to the bank and stood in the shadow of the trees looking across the harbour towards the city. A skiff was a couple of hundred yards off shore coming directly for them. The boy stood looking at it for a moment, studying the rhythmical dipping of the oars, and then watching as the bow sliced neatly through the water. It looked like there were two men in the boat. The one on the oars was young and blond, and the man in the bow had reddish hair and broad shoulders.

Then it struck him like a blow. Stinger and Darnby! They were coming to the camp!

Jamie backed away, his heart pounding. "Meg!" he whispered urgently, never taking his eyes off the incoming boat.

"What is it?"

"It's Darnby and Stinger. They're heading this way. They're coming to the camp!"

Meg grasped Jamie's hand, and they crept forward until they could see the skiff and the two people in it. There was no doubt now. Darnby was standing up in the bow scanning the shore. He was dressed in his usual casual clothes of an open-necked shirt and colourful waistcoat. Stinger was wearing his outfit of scruffy ripped shirt and pants held up with broad suspenders.

"We've got to hide!" Jamie whispered urgently. "We can't let them catch us here."

Doubled over they half ran, half crawled through the camp and back towards the big willow. Then they doubled back through the underbrush to a tall bunch of reeds. From there they could see the camp and the beach but still stay undercover. They settled down into the hiding place just as the skiff reached shore.

A moment later Darnby was standing on the embankment studying the camp. "There's nobody here," he called. When Stinger came to stand beside him he added, "What did I tell you? They've deserted the place and left it all for us."

Stinger looked behind him and then walked cautiously into the camp. With his boot he stirred around the blankets and then bent down and came up with the remnants of a loaf of bread. "They was here last night."

"You sure?"

"This bread is still fresh."

"But I thought you said that the boys were ordered by the judge to stay at the Newsboys' Home."

"They were. It's hard to say if they was here for awhile yesterday afternoon or if they slept here last night and went off to deliver papers this morning. All I know is that we should get outa here as fast as we can."

"Relax, Stinger. Relax. As they used to say in the circus: if you rush a trick, things always go bad." He started heading towards the bush. "Come on. It's this way towards the big willow." They walked towards the tree on what was now a well-worn path.

Jamie and Meg could barely breathe. They were crouched down on their knees peering at Stinger and Darnby through the reeds and concentrating on not making a sound or movement.

"I just hope the stuff is still there," they heard Stinger say. "That kid Jamie was too curious for my likin'."

"They couldn't find this, Stinger. Didn't I tell you this was the perfect hiding place?" Darnby seemed almost reckless.

Meg and Jamie couldn't see very well, but it looked like Darnby was heading right for the willow with Stinger trailing behind. Then they disappeared into the underbrush completely.

"That's it. She's in the big tree," they heard Darnby say. "Boost me up a little, Stinger. By God she's heavy. That's it. Just a little more now. There, I got it. Hold me a moment more until I get it out."

"Good thing you're an acrobat, Darnby."

"Now let me down. Easy now. Good. Let's take her back to the camp so we can get a look."

A moment later the two of them came through the underbrush and into the camp clearing again. Darnby carried the big brown canvas sack and was talking in a loud voice. "Didn't I tell you that was a good hiding place, Stinger? Those kids are too stupid to have found it." His round, freckled face was flushed with excitement.

"Open it up," Stinger urged. "Let's see inside."

"Patience, boy. Everything's here. The sack's as heavy as when I put it in there. Our days of scratchin' out a livin' are over."

"I didn't think it was going to happen, Darnby. Really I didn't. You're too smart for them."

"Them kids and the police are as thick as tree stumps. Often the big willow trees are hollow, and if you can find the right opening you could hide a whole blacksmith's shop in there." He laughed. "Now all that's left is for us to sail across the lake and we've fooled the police and those kids. We've even cut out Murphy's share. Everything will be for us. It's perfect."

"Let's see what's inside the bag," said Stinger excitedly.

"We should be going. We've got a lot of rowing to do if we're to get across the lake by night."

"I want to see inside." The big boy was standing in front of Darnby with his hands on his hips.

"But, Stinger, we don't have time."

"I wanna see. I wanna see everything." He was insistent. "I wanna see everything that's in that bag." Stinger stood in front of Darnby as if riveted to the spot.

"Well, all right. But let's do it fast. We've got to get out of here."

The two of them kneeled over the bag. Darnby undid the cord that held it shut and began pulling out furs. "Look at that," he said almost reverently. "Look at that — mink, muskrat. That one's a beaver pelt. She's a beauty."

From their hiding place Jamie and Meg could see Stinger picking each pelt up carefully and stroking it. Then he said, "Let's see the other stuff."

"Come on, Stinger. We've got to get going."

"No! I want to see everything."

Reluctantly Darnby emptied the sack. There was silverware and several heavy candlestick holders. At the very bottom was jewellery studded with precious stones.

Stinger's face glowed with pleasure and greed. "Look at it all. We's gonna be rich, ain't we, Darnby. Rich!" The trembling excitement in his voice reached all the way to Meg and Jamie. "I ain't never had nothin' like this. We's gonna be rich and live in a big house and have servants and cooks and everything." A crazy smile was on his face. "Maybe I could have a dog. Think I could have a dog, Darnby? A dog just of my very own. One that would follow me around everywhere and … and be mine."

"Sure, kid, sure. You want yerself a dog then you can have one, but let's get out of here before every policeman in Toronto discovers us."

Stinger did not seem to hear. "I ain't never had a dog, you know. I've always been by myself. Just me, Stinger, alone. And now I'm going to have my very own dog."

Darnby was beginning to get impatient. "Come on, Stinger. We've got to get going. Help me get these furs back into the bag."

But the boy paid no attention. "We'll have a big house with a yard and servants and everythin'."

"Stinger!" Darnby shouted. "Enough! Let's get moving." The boy seemed to snap out of his dream and bent into the job of stuffing the furs back into the bag.

"The boat," Jamie whispered to his sister. "We've got to get one of the boats and go and warn Moffat before it's too late. Maybe we should take both of them and then they would be stranded here on the island."

Jamie looked back at the two figures. Darnby was stuffing the furs back into the bag while Stinger handed the pelts to him.

With a nod of his head the boy backed out from his position in the reeds and began creeping along, fully crouched over.

The water's edge was not far. Meg was right behind him. Jamie glanced back. Darnby and Stinger were almost finished. There was an open spot before the beach and the boats. Jamie paused. Again he glanced back. There was no time to lose. He made a quick dash across the open stretch, over the small embankment and found himself crouching beside Darnby's boat. A moment later Meg was beside him, panting hard.

Carefully they peeked over the bank. Stinger and Darnby were standing up now. Stinger was holding the opening of the brown canvas sack while Darnby tied it with a strong cord.

There were only seconds left. Bending over, Jamie went around to the other side of the skiff and began to push it out from its resting spot behind the fallen log into deep water. Now the boat was riding free. The boy motioned for Meg to get in and she slipped over the side.

"I'm going for the other boat," he whispered.

"Be careful!"

Again he looked over the bank. Stinger and Darnby were standing up, talking. Jamie began to run along the beach towards the other boat hunched over so that the bank blocked him from view.

At the boat his breath was coming in short gasps and his heart pounded. Without pause he grabbed the bow and began pushing the skiff into the open water. It rubbed against the sand, then floated free. He launched himself up over the side. Water splashed. An oar knocked loudly against the gunwales.

"Hey, what's goin' on here?" It was Darnby standing on the bank, a shocked look on his face.

"You ain't gonna get away with that!" shouted Stinger in a high-pitched voice.

Jamie scrambled to get the oars. He had to get away!

Stinger launched himself across the beach and into the water. Splashes flew as he ran. His eyes were wild. An animal-like cry came from his lips.

Jamie had the oars and with an enormous pull he launched the skiff out onto the water. It skidded away. Again he dug the oars into the water and pulled with all his strength.

But Stinger pursued him. Water splashed up to his knees and his thighs. Then with one powerful lurching dive the big boy threw himself at the skiff and caught it with each hand clutching onto the board at the very stern.

Violently Jamie kicked at the hands, but with a massive effort Stinger pulled his body through the water and launched himself up over the stern and into the bottom of the boat.

Dropping the oars, Jamie frantically grappled with the wet figure, trying to push him over the side and back into the water again, but suddenly his legs went out from under him as Stinger's strong arms swept him down. In a moment he was underneath this powerful raging beast of muscle, bone and brawn.

Stinger was bearing down on his chest with his full weight. His eyes were wild; his mouth opened in a soundless roar. Now a knife was in his hand — a long gleaming weapon that glinted in the sunshine.

Jamie struggled to get away. His arms flailed but it did no good. Stinger held the knife high above his head, ready to plunge down.

"Let me go!" Jamie shouted. He struggled, twisting his body with all the strength he had left.

Momentarily Stinger was thrown off balance. Then he reached down and put a hammerlock around Jamie's neck. He rolled him over onto his stomach and then yanked his head back with such strength that Jamie thought his spine would break. Then the boy could feel the razor-sharp blade digging into his jugular vein.

"Good work!" said Darnby from the shore. "My God, Stinger, you could get a job in the circus. That was the fastest capture ever."

"Meg!" Stinger shouted. "Meg, come back with that boat now!" He forced Jamie to his feet, the knife digging painfully into the boy's flesh.

Meg was a few yards off shore. She could easily get away. For a moment she paused.

"Go!" Jamie suddenly shouted. "Warn Moffat!" Then Stinger pulled back on his neck hard, and the boy collapsed to his knees in pain.

Stinger was panting. "If you go, Meg, you ain't never seeing your brother again!"

Without a word Meg dipped the oars into the water and drew the boat back to shore.

CHAPTER 17

WE got 'em now, Stinger," Darnby gloated. "Hain't the whole business fallin' into place? We got our loot and we got our enemies, too. What could be better?"

Stinger suddenly let go of Jamie and pushed him hard. The boy fell into the stern of the boat. He lay there rubbing his neck and chest until slowly the white-hot pain began to subside.

"Who's this girl?" Darnby suddenly asked.

"It's the kid's sister, Meg. They're both nothin' but trouble. I say we should do 'em in."

"I don't know, Stinger. They might be useful yet."

"How's that?"

"We're headin' across the lake to the U.S. side. It might be worthwhile to hold them as a bit of insurance. Anyway, they can help row. That'll give them something to do, and if there is any problem, well, we'll deal with them then."

"I don't like it," Stinger said. "This kid Jamie's given me nothin' but trouble from the first time I met him."

"But he might be useful. Think of it that way." Then Darnby began giving out orders. "We're going to take my boat. It's a little bigger and should handle the waves better. Get the mast up and rig the sails. The sooner we get out of here the better."

"I'm not helping you get away," Jamie said sullenly.

"No?" A cruel smile came across Stinger's face. He held his knife up so the boy could see it. "You're going to help or I'll split you from stem to gizzard. Now get out of there and help me rig this boat."

Jamie and Meg exchanged glances. What could they do now?

The two boys wrestled the mast and boom from under the seats and then hauled out the canvas that was folded and stored under the deck in front. They fitted the boom onto the mast and laced the sail to it, ready to run up the mast when it was needed. Then they managed to stand it up and get it into the fittings near the bow.

Jamie worked slowly and clumsily. Several times Stinger cursed him for taking so long. Still, even with his delays, it was no more than ten minutes before the sail was rigged.

Darnby had been standing on the beach holding an extra pair of oars and watching the boys work. When they were finished, he said, "We'll set the sail once we get into the open waters of the lake. Let's get moving. There's a lot of water to put under us before we reach a safe harbour."

The two sets of oars were fitted into place. Darnby got into the stern beside the tiller with the canvas bag, the boys were at the oars and Meg sat in the bow with her long dress gathered under her. Stinger pushed with his oar in the sand until they floated free and then with a couple of strokes they left the shadows of the trees and were into the open water.

It was mid-morning and already the fierce sun beat down, glaring off the surface of the water. The vivid blue of the sky seemed dark and threatening, yet there was not a cloud. Only the hot yellow sun, like a burning disc suspended in the sky.

Darnby was in high spirits. "We're off to the United States with a fortune in our bag. Hain't we too smart for them all, Stinger, too smart."

The big blond boy smiled. "Them coppers don't know nothin', they're so stupid. We had the loot just sittin' there in the tree all that time and they couldn't even find it."

"How did you two meet up again?" Jamie could not help asking.

"We had that figured out long before anyone was ever captured. Didn't we, Stinger?"

"Yeah. We had this here secret agreement that if we ever got separated we would meet at an old mill on the Humber River. I knew Darnby would be waiting for me, so as soon as I got out of court yesterday I went down to the harbour and got the skiff and rowed right there. When I found him I knew we was gonna be home free. We'd get the stuff and everythin' would work out just right."

Darnby laughed. "What a scheme. The whole thing couldn't have worked out better if we had planned it."

"Yeah," Stinger agreed. "Now all we got to do is get across to that there United States and the Toronto police can't touch us. We's gonna live the good life, ain't we, Darnby? It's gonna be a big house with servants and I'm gonna get my own dog and everythin'."

"Sure, Stinger, sure. Now bend your backs into those oars, fellers. The open lake's not far ahead. Then we'll put up the sail and drift over to the other side easy as a cloud."

They had rowed out from shore and were heading towards the Eastern Gap and the waters of Lake Ontario. Jamie was on one set of oars, but he only made a pretense of rowing. Stinger sat farther to the stern and bent into the work, but the boat was heavy and the four people in it made it even heavier. Despite all of Stinger's efforts it moved sluggishly.

"Row," Darnby called out. "Come on, you two. Move this boat. We've got a long way to go before we're safe."

They were beginning to round the end of the island and as the boat entered the Gap they began feeling the motion of the waves from the lake. Jamie turned to look at the distant horizon. It was a long way across to the other side.

The sun, glaring off the blue surface of the water, made the boy squint painfully. The heat of the day burned, grinding into his skull until he felt a huge pressure just behind his eyes. It was a terrible wrenching, splitting feeling.

How could they ever get away? Already it was too far to swim back to the island. Soon the land would recede behind them and they would be in the middle of Lake Ontario with two outlaws. Would they even survive?

Suddenly around the end of the island and into the Gap came a big white mackinaw boat with four men at the oars and one at the tiller. Jamie felt his heart leap. It was the police! Detective Moffat was coming to get them!

For a moment the boy was going to cry out, but he bit his tongue. He let his oars drag in the water, not even pretending to be rowing. Rapidly the police boat closed in on them.

Then Stinger was shouting, "It's the coppers! Darnby, it's the coppers! Where did they come from?"

"What? It can't be!"

"It is! I tell you it's the coppers!"

The big boat was sweeping down on them swiftly now. It could handle the swells of the open lake better than the skiff, and the long oars dipped into the water without pause.

"Row!" Darnby shouted. "You beat them in a race before. You can do it again."

But Jamie had no intention of rowing this time. He let his oars drag in the water.

"Bend into them oars, Jamie!" Darnby shouted, and the boy felt Stinger give him a sharp clip across the side of his head. It changed nothing. Now he was even pushing back on the oars, countering the motion of the boat. The police rapidly closed in on them.

"You're not rowing," Stinger shrieked. He dropped an oar and turned to hit the boy again. Jamie easily dodged out of the way.

The police were less than a hundred yards away. The big men on the oars were bending into the effort. Moffat was standing by the tiller urging them on.

Meg had found a spare paddle and put it out to drag in the water. Suddenly the skiff began to turn off course. Stinger stood up and swung his fist hard at her but she ducked out of the way. The police were sweeping down on them.

"It's them two kids!" Stinger shrieked. "We should have done them in back at the camp! Should have drowned them like rats!"

Darnby was standing up in the stern of the boat, his face red. "The police hain't gonna get this loot. I don't care what it costs me!" He lifted the canvas bag over his head. A contorted look came over his face. "Let the lake claim it all!" he shouted and then hurled the bag as far as he could out into the water.

Jamie watched, paralyzed. The canvas bag arched through the air and splashed heavily into the lake. It bobbed for a moment, turned on its side and began sinking beneath the waves.

The stolen property would be lost forever. How could he redeem himself with the judge if he didn't recover the loot? How could he convince him that he was anything but a common thief?

Suddenly the boy scrambled onto the seat of the boat and dove over the side, his body arching gracefully as he sliced cleanly into a wave. A second later he broke the surface and began to swim to where the bag had gone down.

A wave caught him and he choked. Jamie had never swum in open water like this and he floundered for a moment, but he pressed on, putting one hand in front of the other, desperate to keep afloat and find the bag.

He sucked in a deep gulp of air and dove. Down he went like a stone — using his arms, kicking his feet — his shoes and clothing dragging him down into the cold depths of the lake.

He kept his eyes open, searching for the bag. The sun streamed through the dark waters in long yellow rays that stabbed into the depths. His arms thrashed, and the deeper he went the more his ears throbbed in pain. He kicked his feet, fighting to go down.

But then he felt it. The rough canvas surface of the bag rasped against his hand. The heavy bag was sinking slowly into the depths.

Jamie could feel the rope Damby had tied around the opening. He grasped it at the top, swung his body around and began swimming for the surface. By God, it was heavy! He kicked his legs and flailed with his arms but didn't seem to be moving to the surface at all. Now the boy's ears were bursting. He was starved for air, but he couldn't give up.

Violently he kicked and swam with his one free arm. His strength seemed to be giving out. In one last frantic effort he tried to hike the bag up to the surface, but it only seemed to drag him down. Now he had to get air.

In a desperate effort to save himself, he left the bag and swam for the surface. His head was pounding. His lungs pained. Finally, he burst into the air and gulped in long greedy gasps.

Again he took a deep breath and dove. Down he went, sinking into the cool depths of the water as he churned with his arms and legs. Again his hands felt the canvas. He grasped the top of the bag and looked up to see the sun penetrating through the water like a beacon.

His muscles ached and his lungs pained from lack of oxygen. Then he felt himself become light headed and drowsy. A soft mellow feeling came over him, inviting him to drift into unconsciousness — to slip into the gloomy depths of a watery grave.

Things were blurring. His swimming became slower and slower. It was all he could do to hold onto the bag. A floating, watery dream seemed about to reach up and take him.

Suddenly, unexpectedly, he broke the surface of the water. A gentle wave slapped his face, and he drew in a sudden gulp. Water caught in his throat, he began to cough and then retched. His whole body was contorting, but he had the canvas bag in a vice-like grip.

"Jamie! Jamie! Are you all right?" he heard his sister call to him. He held up his hand weakly and then struggled to see what was happening.

Stinger had his arm around Meg's neck, pressing his knife to her throat. The two of them were standing up in the stern of the skiff. The big mackinaw boat drifted just beyond them as the police tried to decide what to do.

"Stay away!" Stinger shouted. "Stay away, coppers, or I'll throttle this girl and drop her into the lake." He sounded like he had gone completely mad. "Bunch of lousy no-good coppers. I hate you all! Could have had a house of my own with servants and a dog and everything ... "

"Don't harm that girl, Stinger!" Moffat ordered.

"Get away from me, you coppers! We're gettin' out of here. We're sailin' across the lake and we ain't never comin' back."

Jamie had been swimming towards the skiff, dragging the heavy sack after him. Suddenly he shouted, "You leave my sister alone!"

Stinger was distracted. His head whirled around to see who was there, and he loosened his grip on Meg's throat. Quickly she twisted sideways, dropped her shoulder into his rib cage and heaved against him with all her might. Stinger lost his balance, caught his feet in the ribbing of the boat and then fell heavily overboard.

"Get him, quick!" Moffat shouted. "And someone get Jamie!" Two men launched themselves over the side of the mackinaw and in three powerful strokes one was at Jamie's side.

"This boy's got the sack of stolen goods here," he shouted.

Moffat seemed surprised. "You mean the sack Darnby threw overboard?"

"Yeah, and it's as heavy as lead."

"That was some swimming. Bring it aboard. Looks like we've got this whole business all tidied up," the detective said proudly. "You're under arrest. All of you."

CHAPTER 18

"ALL right. Over the side now." The two policemen still in the boat reached down, grabbed Stinger under the arms and heaved him over the gunwales and into the bottom of the mackinaw boat.

"You next, Jamie."

The boy struggled to bring the heavy sack to the side of the boat. One of the policemen hauled it aboard. Then they brought Jamie over the side and helped the two policemen. After Darnby and Meg joined them they were all assembled.

Moffat sat in the stern of the boat sorting through the contents of the big brown bag. He took out fur pelts, trinkets and jewellery. "Looks like all the fur is here and some other things taken in earlier break-ins, but there are still a lot of things missing."

The detective stared at Jamie with a puzzled look. "Why did you risk your life to save this stuff?"

"I guess … I wanted to get it back … to the owners." Jamie paused for a moment and then added, "I wanted to show the judge that I wasn't a criminal." Jamie shivered with cold and exhaustion.

The detective shook his head. "I don't believe that. Just a half hour ago you and your sister were all set to sail away with Darnby and Stinger."

"No, that's not the way it was."

"Then what tall story do you have for us, Jamie? I might as well hear all the lies at once."

The policemen had attached the skiff to the stern of the mackinaw boat and began rowing back to the Eastern Gap and Toronto Harbour. Stinger and Darnby both sat dejected as they listened.

"Yesterday, after we were let go, Meg and I came over to the island with Bud and Paddy," Jamie explained. "We looked for the loot again but couldn't find it. Afterwards Bud and Paddy went back to the city, and we slept overnight at the camp. Then, this morning, Stinger and Darnby showed up. They had the bag hidden in the big tree. They got it and were going to head off across the lake. We tried to stop them, but they forced us into the boat and were going to take us with them."

Moffat shook his head. "Not very convincing."

"But it's true. Ask Meg."

"Why should I believe her? The two of you were in this together. You were trying to escape with Stinger and Darnby."

"That doesn't make sense," said Meg, trying to stay calm. "If we were trying to escape why did Stinger hold me hostage like that?"

"Stinger's crazy. Everyone knows that. He'd have done that to anyone if he thought he could save his own skin." Then the detective leaned forward. "Look, this is how I see it. The two of you were involved from the beginning and you were trying to escape with them across the lake."

"No! That's not right." Panic flooded over Jamie.

Moffat only smiled cynically. "Did you know that I arranged to have you released from jail yesterday?"

Jamie was puzzled. "You had us released … "

"I wanted to clear up this case and as long as you and the others were in jail I figured we would never find Darnby or recover the stolen property. I arranged to have you released to see what direction you would run."

"What direction we would run?"

"That's right. My partner here was detailed to follow Stinger. Right after court the boy headed down to the wharf and got your other skiff and rowed west. Stinger went all the way down to the Humber River and then up as far as the old mill where Darnby was waiting for him."

"You followed me?" asked Stinger, shocked. "You mean, like, someone followed me in another boat?"

"Well, it wasn't quite as simple as that. Our man was on a bicycle and he followed you from shore. It was hard at first but once you were going up the Humber it was easy."

Darnby shook his head in disbelief. "You mean you spotted us both at the mill?"

"That's right. We could have arrested you last night, but we wanted to see what your next move would be. It was a gamble that we took and one that paid off handsomely, because it led back to these two young criminals right here."

"But you've got it all wrong," said Jamie.

"I don't think so. This morning as soon as it was light Darnby and Stinger came down the Humber in the skiff. Once in the lake they turned east. It was obvious they were heading for the camp where the two of you were waiting for them. Our man came back to police headquarters and by the time we got our officers organized and our boat out you were already making your escape. If we hadn't appeared you would have been halfway across the lake by now."

"But that's not the way it was."

"Then what is it I left out, my little thief?"

"Stinger and Darnby forced us to go with them."

"I suppose you're going to tell me again that you didn't know where the stuff was hidden, and you just happened to be there when they came along."

"Yes, that's the way it was. They forced us into the boat. Darnby said I could help them row across the lake, and he thought we would be a type of insurance for them."

But even as he talked, Jamie could see that Moffat did not believe him. He had to find another way to convince him of the story. But how?

It had been an effort to persuade the detective to go along with their plan, but late that afternoon Jamie walked up Jarvis Street with a note in his hand. The alleyway where the Boar's Head Tavern was located was narrow and dirty. The boy couldn't help thinking that it was an appropriate place for the red-faced Irishman.

He found the caretaker and left the note with him. It was a simple message.

Murphy:

We have some things for you. Meet us at 10:00 tonight on Taylor's Wharf.

                                    Jamie and Meg Bains

Now they were waiting. Paddy and Bud sat on the hull of an overturned rowboat, Meg was in the shadows, leaning up against the wheel of a deserted wagon, and Jamie perched cross-legged on one of the boxes where they had sheltered from the rain that night so long ago. No one said a word.

The burning hot day had died in a bright flame of sunset. In the west some clouds were still tinged a blood red but the rest of the sky was almost in darkness. Venus was fast sinking into the horizon and above them stars were appearing, one at a time, looking like crystal diamonds in the vast dome. As the heat of the day began to lift, a slight inshore breeze flowed across them like a gentle breath, but the water remained undisturbed, a dark mirror making perfect reflections of the light.

Jamie stirred. Was Murphy going to come? Would the big Irishman even bother with them?

The boy looked across the harbour to the island. It was no more than a dark mound that bulged out of the water a half a mile away. He wondered if he would ever see it again.

Someone was coming! The boy heard the crunch of footsteps in the gravel and the hum of a popular tune. A big man was striding along the railway tracks. In the dim light the boy could see the shape of a round bowler hat and a tweed jacket flapping open. Suddenly a cigar in the man's mouth glowed a fiery red, revealing the whiskered face of John Murphy.

As the Irishman walked onto the dock Jamie slid off his perch onto the wooden deck. He stood waiting.

"Well, sure if it isn't Jamie Bains out here coolin' off from the hot Toronto summer. Where is that no-account sister of yours?"

When Meg appeared silently out of the darkness he continued his patter. "Ah, there you are, girl, as much trouble as ever, I suspect."

Bud and Paddy came to stand with the others. "And I suppose these little street urchins are your partners in crime. Is that the truth?"

Jamie felt a tight ball of nervousness in his stomach. "Yes, Murphy. We all work together."

"And where's Darnby and that other lad, Stinger? What happened to them?"

"They were going to double-cross you."

"What ... ?" Murphy leaned towards the boy. Jamie could smell the whisky on his breath. "What do you mean, double- cross?"

"They had some stolen furs, and they were going to sail across to Rochester and cut you out altogether."

"Cut me out? Why would they want to do that? I give a good price to all me customers."

As Jamie continued talking his confidence grew. "But we stopped them, Mr. Murphy. We got the goods right here, and we'd like to sell them to you ourselves."

"But how did you get them?"

The boy smiled. "Let's just say that when they sailed away they ended up empty handed, and now we've got the stuff."

Murphy pulled the cigar from his mouth. Slowly a smile spread across his face. "Tricked them, did you? Bejesus, maybe I underestimated you and that sister of yours. I had you figured as honest citizens, but maybe I was wrong. Now let's see the stuff you've got."

Jamie reached into the shadows beside the boxes and hauled out the canvas bag stuffed to overflowing.

"Let me see it, lad."

Quickly Jamie pulled it back and put it between him and Meg. "We want to talk prices first."

"Prices? How can I talk prices before I've seen the merchandise?"

"You don't even get to see the stuff unless we know we're going to get a good price."

Murphy looked annoyed. "Look, lad. I pay the highest prices for stolen goods in town, and I give out good hard cash. Ever since I got to Toronto there's been a wave of robberies because I've been paying top dollar. If these are the furs and jewellery that I heard Darnby was getting then you're going to make a pretty penny."

"How much? We want to know."

"One-third of its value. That's what I pay. One-third. You won't get a better price anywhere. Now give me the bag and let me see the stuff."

He leaned forward, but just as he was about to grasp it a harsh voice came from behind. "So you're the big man in town, Murphy. You're the reason for this crime wave."

"What?" Murphy whirled around. "Who's that? Who's there?"

"Toronto police. You're under arrest!"

"What ... ?" Murphy was in a panic.

"Theft! Possession of stolen property!" Moffat barked out. "The whole business. We're going to throw the book at you."

"I've been tricked. Bejesus, I've been foiled by this young no-account of a boy!"

"Get him!" Moffat and the big constable with him both made a lunge, but Murphy was too fast. He had Jamie by the front of the shirt and was yelling.

"I'll get you, boy! I'll get you!"

But now a virtual hoard had attacked the Irishman. The two policemen grabbed him from behind, Meg stomped on Murphy's foot, Paddy pushed him in the stomach and even little Bud kicked him in the shins. In a moment the big man's arms where shackled behind his back, and he was helpless.

"Murphy, you're going to be out of circulation for a long time," said the detective.

When the meaning of what had happened sank in, Meg hugged her brother. But then they saw Moffat watching them, his hands on his hips and a serious look still on his face.

"What will happen to us now?" Jamie asked, suddenly uncertain of himself again.

"I have to admit that you did fine work tonight. If it wasn't for you I don't know when we would have caught Murphy, and he turned out to be the big fish in this whole operation. But that doesn't free you from your own crimes."

"Doesn't this change anything?" asked Meg in disbelief.

"Guilty. That's what the courts will say. All three of you boys are guilty of serious crimes of theft. There's no way around that."

A silence fell on the group. The dark night was filled with shadows. Overhead the sky was filled with stars.

"But maybe," the detective began again, "maybe you have shown that you have learned from your mistakes. I will see to it that these charges are dropped, but only on certain conditions. Bud and Paddy, you will have to live in the Newsboys' Home until you are old enough to get regular jobs."

He paused for a moment. "And, Jamie. I'll give you until sunset tomorrow night to get out of the city. If you're not gone I'll see to it that you pay the full penalty for these crimes."

"But that's not fair."

"It's the way it's going to be."

Without another word Moffat turned, joined the policeman guarding Murphy, and the three walked back towards the city.

For a moment Jamie looked out across the water to the island, now only a darkened mound, and then at the city gleaming with lights. He didn't want to leave.

Then Meg touched her brother's hand. "We'll be all right, Jamie. West of here is Hamilton, London, Windsor. We'll find something somewhere."

The boy smiled and sighed. "Maybe you're right. At least … at least we'll be free to start again."